When it's more than just friends...

"I have a long weekend for the holiday," Zac said. "I've got to check in at the market tomorrow morning, but the rest of the day is mine. What if I come pick you up and take you to lunch?"

"Zac, you must have better things to do," Eli insisted.

"You say that every time I ask to spend time with you. Since my sister is convinced we can talk without actually speaking, just like my parents can, want to guess what I'm saying without saying?"

Eli tried to look serious, but all she could do was laugh. That seemed to be a common theme with Zac. They talked, they enjoyed each other's company and they both laughed a lot.

"Okay, tomorrow for lunch." She opened the car door.

Before she got out, Zac leaned over and kissed her cheek. It was light, platonic even, and yet she felt a bit breathless in a way that had nothing to do with the blast of cold air that flooded the car.

"Uh, well, thanks for a lovely day, Zac. I'd really best get going."

And in his eyes, without him saying a word, she could see that he knew his light kiss on the cheek had flustered her, and that he was pleased.

She brushed a fingertip over the spot.

What was she going to do about Zac Keller?

Dear Reader,

This year is Harlequin's 60th Anniversary! Being part of the Harlequin family always was and is a dream of mine.

As my youngest child got older, I realized that one day soon she would go to school...and I'd need to go back to work. The question was, what did I want to do? This very quiet little whisper niggled around the edges of my mind...I'd like to write. And so I started writing. And submitting. And being rejected. In January of 2000 I was ready to admit defeat. I told my husband it was time to go look for a job. He told me no. We were fine financially and he was positive I'd sell to Harlequin Books. I just had to keep trying, and he was willing to do whatever it took to help. (Is it any wonder I write romance, with him as an example of what a hero should be?)

Two months later a woman called and introduced herself as Kathryn Lye...and bought my first Harlequin book, *I Waxed My Legs for This?* Three months after that, Allison Lyons from Silhouette Romance bought *Do You Hear What I Hear?* Nine years later this book, my twenty-eighth romance for Harlequin, is hitting the shelves and I'm struck by the fact that I am living my dream. That's such a rare and wonderful thing.

So many dreams don't live up to their hype, but my dream of working with Harlequin Books has been so much more than I ever imagined it could be. I've encountered the most amazing people, traveled all over the country and met so many truly lovely readers and other writers. I am so lucky.

So happy anniversary, Harlequin! May your stories of love keep touching the hearts of readers for years and years to come!

Holly Jacobs

Unexpected Gifts
Holly Jacobs

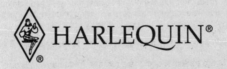

TORONTO • NEW YORK • LONDON
AMSTERDAM • PARIS • SYDNEY • HAMBURG
STOCKHOLM • ATHENS • TOKYO • MILAN • MADRID
PRAGUE • WARSAW • BUDAPEST • AUCKLAND

Recycling programs
for this product may
not exist in your area.

ISBN-13: 978-0-373-78346-5

UNEXPECTED GIFTS

Copyright © 2009 by Holly Fuhrmann.

Printed in U.S.A.

ABOUT THE AUTHOR

In 2000, Holly Jacobs sold her first book to Harlequin Enterprises. She's since sold more than twenty-five novels to the publisher. Her romances have won numerous awards and made the Waldenbooks bestseller list. In 2005, Holly won a prestigious Career Achievement Award from *Romantic Times BOOKreviews.* In her nonwriting life Holly is married to a police captain, and together they have four children. Visit Holly at www.HollyJacobs.com, or you can snail-mail her at P.O. Box 11102, Erie, PA 16514-1102.

Books by Holly Jacobs

HARLEQUIN SUPERROMANCE
1511—SAME TIME NEXT SUMMER

HARLEQUIN AMERICAN ROMANCE
1232—ONCE UPON A THANKSGIVING
1238—ONCE UPON A CHRISTMAS
1247—ONCE UPON A VALENTINE'S

HARLEQUIN EVERLASTING
THE HOUSE ON BRIAR HILL ROAD

For all the amazing teachers who work in the
Erie School District's Teen Parenting Program,
especially Jeanne Bender, Mary Fuhrmann,
Connie Sementilli and Bonnie Sobeck. Thanks
for letting me be a part of the amazing work
you do. You have touched so many students'
lives, and the ripple effects from your work
will be felt for years to come.

And for Sharon Lorei, who was an
"Eli Cartwright" sort of teacher in my life.

PROLOGUE

"There's no way to cheat nature."
—*Pregnancy, Childbirth and Parenting for Teens,* by Mary Jeanne Lorei

ARIEL MAYORS KNEW that, until recently, she'd been teacher's pet. A favorite. The student who could do no wrong.

She'd cultivated that status with the same care that a gardener used looking after prized orchids. By the time Ariel had reached her senior year of high school she'd practically perfected the art of perfect. She was always the first one to raise her hand, the first one to volunteer and almost always the best student in class.

Popularity was a game that she didn't just play with the teachers, she played it with fellow students as well.

To garner the girls' admiration she made sure she never poached boyfriends, that she always offered a shoulder in any cry-worthy moment and that she was never without an extra Tampax in her purse for those time-of-the-month emergencies.

She'd discovered the basic truth that once you'd borrowed a tampon from someone, it was hard to hate them.

Ariel was a cheerleader, which provided her a ready-made social group, and also meant she was one of the girls all the boys wanted to date. She knew this part of her popularity didn't stem from any planning of hers. Biology had blessed her with blond hair and a long, lithe body. But she'd worked at the rest—worked on knowing what clothes to wear, how to apply makeup flawlessly. She worked at knowing when to laugh, when to draw closer, when to pull back.

Well, she thought, she'd known when to pull back until that one night in Charlie Markowski's Lumina van.

She stood in front of Ms. Cartwright's desk. Her teacher wasn't beautiful, but there was something appealing about her average-ness. Brown shoulder-length hair, blue eyes. A little shorter than Ariel's five feet, six inches. Ms. Cartwright was the kind of person who was so normal-looking she could easily get lost in a crowd in a way Ariel never could. That was, until she smiled. Then Ms. Cartwright was beautiful. Ariel wasn't sure how that worked, she just knew it did. She wanted to be like Ms. Cartwright someday. Calm, collected—a woman in charge of her own destiny. Someone who got more beautiful when they smiled.

Only Ms. Cartwright wasn't smiling today.

"Ariel," Ms. Cartwright said, disappointment right there in that one word and echoing so fiercely in her favorite teacher's expression.

Ariel had disappointed so many people in the last few weeks. She'd worked so hard to please this one woman, and now, she'd disappointed her, too.

"Ariel, Mrs. Brown came to see me. She says she found this in your book." Ms. Cartwright slid the small piece of paper across the desk. "Is this crib note yours?"

"Yes," Ariel whispered.

"Pardon?"

"Yes."

"Do you have an explanation?"

"I worked at the restaurant last night and

planned on studying during my break but Dale, the dork manager at Barney's, wouldn't give me one. We had a bus come in and…" She simply shrugged. What more was there to say? She'd done it—she'd cheated. She could add that to her growing list of descriptions.

Cheerleader.

Student council rep.

Straight A student.

Pregnant teen.

Cheater.

Ms. Cartwright didn't yell, didn't scream. She just shook her head sadly and asked, "Do you really think this is the way to handle things? By taking the easy way out?"

"I just didn't know what else to do."

"Did it occur to you that you could go to Mrs. Brown and explain the situation to her. Or, you could have come to me. It's part of my job description…helping you find options. There are always some. I know you're new to the program, but it's pretty much our mantra—finding options." She sighed. "Listen, Ariel, this stopped being about you when you became pregnant. You will be this baby's role model. He or she will look to you to see how to live. Is this what you'd want *your* child to do? Do you want them to take the easy way out?"

"No. I didn't think of it like that."

"You have to learn to think about everything you do in that way—how it will affect your baby. You need to do what's best for them, always. Even when it's difficult for you. Now, how do you think we should handle this?"

"You know, those are the kinds of questions all us kids hate. You make us decide on a fair punishment."

"I make you take responsibility for your actions. Most teens have a few more years to learn about actions and consequences—the girls in this program don't have the luxury of time. *You* don't have that luxury."

She looked pointedly at Ariel's stomach and the barely there baby bump.

"Ariel, I see so much potential in you. Don't blow it. If you have a problem, come see me, see Mrs. Brown. There are people here for you. Don't forget that."

"Maybe I should start by writing an apology to Mrs. Brown?"

"I think that's an excellent place to begin. Come see me tomorrow and we'll talk about what else you think is required in order to make this right."

Darn. Ariel had hoped that a letter of apology would be all that she had to do to smooth this over. Obviously, it wasn't.

"Okay, I'll think about it and see you tomorrow." She practically sprang for the door, anxious to escape Ms. Cartwright's sympathetic gaze. It would be easier if the teacher would get pissed off and yell. But no, not her, she only looked as if her girls screwing up hurt her.

Ariel turned the doorknob, and pushed at the door, ready to make her escape when Ms. Cartwright's voice stopped her. "And Ariel?"

She turned back and saw pain in Ms. Cartwright's smile. She'd do almost anything to replace that look of disappointment with one of pride.

"You can't cheat nature. You are going to be a mother in a few months and there are no crib notes that will let you fake your way through being a good parent. And that's what you owe this baby. Being the best parent, the best example you can be."

"Yes, ma'am."

"And for that matter, Ariel, life happens. You can't cheat your way through it, either. There are no crib notes. You have to live each day as well as you can. I'll see you tomorrow."

Finally, dismissed, Ariel hurried away before Ms. Cartwright could say anything else profoundly painful.

There were no crib notes for being a parent. For being an adult.

Ariel desperately wished there were.

CHAPTER ONE

"There are four stages of mourning. Denial. Sadness. Anger. Acceptance. Becoming pregnant in your teens means that some dreams have to be put away, others altered. It's a death of one future. You have to mourn that loss before you can move ahead and plan a new future…one that includes the baby you're carrying."
—*Pregnancy, Childbirth and Parenting for Teens,* by Mary Jeanne Lorei

THERE WAS SOMETHING completely undignified about peeing in a cup. It took a certain knack that Elinore Cartwright didn't feel she had acquired and, to be honest, she didn't know that she wanted to be presented too many more opportunities to develop it.

Despite the fact she was nowhere near a master, she managed the fill the little paper cup. She washed her hands and then, clutching the paper gown at the back, hurried across the hall to her assigned examination room. She hoisted herself back onto the table.

Sitting on paper, wearing paper, covering herself with a square piece of quilted paper. Every movement was a festival noise.

The only nonpaper item she was wearing for her less-than-happily anticipated annual checkup was her wildly striped toe socks. She'd left them on partly because now that it was the end of October, her feet wouldn't be warm again for at least eight months, and partly because she felt they dressed up her paper ensemble.

She sank back onto her paper-shrouded shrine and waited. Right on cue, as her body relaxed, her thoughts picked up steam, tumbling over themselves. There was no flitting involved, just a terrible tangled twist of to-do items and worries.

To-do: Call Zac Keller and set up a meeting for the end of the week.

Ariel Mayor. She replayed their talk from earlier this afternoon. It had seemed to go well. She saw a lot of potential in the girl. As a matter of fact…

To-do: Pull together Ariel's information

and see if Zac would agree that she'd make an excellent test-run for the new Community Action, Teen-parent Apprentice Project.

It had been almost fifteen years since Eli had started the George County School District's teen parenting program. George County was a large, primarily rural county just south of Erie, Pennsylvania. Her job was to find ways to cut the county's number of teen parents, and help those who were pregnant or already parents graduate and go on to be worthwhile members of the community.

The statistics said her program was working. She experienced that warm glow of pride she always felt when she thought about the inroads she'd made.

The number of teen mothers in the county was falling, the number of teen moms who graduated was climbing. And there had been a nice bump in the number of her mothers who went on to college or some type of vocational training after graduation.

This new project was just another way of helping her girls. Partnering local businesses with the students in the program. Giving the teens jobs with flexibility, jobs that would provide crucial work experience.

It sounded as if Ariel was already working hard, too hard, at that restaurant. This program might be just the ticket for her.

And despite Ariel Mayor's slight bump in the road, Eli was determined that this girl would be one of her successes.

Her to-do list was replaced as a niggle of worry crept into the forefront of her thoughts. She'd figured passing so easily from fertility to menopause was a good thing. After half a year of erratic cycles, her periods had just stopped a few months ago with no other problems arising. No hot flashes, mood swings, trouble sleeping.

Eli took this as another sign that her life was pretty much perfect. She had Arthur, who, although he was a little less than exciting, was good company and a dependable boyfriend. She had a job she loved, a great family and good friends. And now, she'd had a pain-free transition into menopause at the ripe old age of forty-four.

At least, that's what she thought until Dr. Benton had asked to run a few tests. One of which involved peeing in that stupid cup.

How long did it take to do whatever voodoo test he was doing? And what did he think was wrong?

Cancer?

That horrible C word.

Cancer of what? Cervix, uterus, ovaries? Maybe that was it, cancer had eaten all her eggs, so her periods had stopped.

She tried to force her thoughts back to her long to-do list. It was much more pleasant.

Okay. To-do…

Her mind was blank. She was saved from trying to fill it though when Dr. Benton opened the door.

"Go ahead and just tell me. Cancer has eaten all my eggs, right?"

He laughed.

Hmm, doctors didn't normally laugh when telling someone they had a cancer, right?

She took a deep breath and let it out slowly, feeling better. She sat up and all the paper crinkled merrily. "I have an active imagination. So what's the news?"

"You're not in menopause—"

"Then it is cancer. Cancer of the uterus? That's why my period stopped."

"You're pregnant."

"Cancer of the cervix?"

"Pregnant. As in going to have a baby."

She laughed. "Funny. Ha ha. You can tell me. Just say the words, I can take it."

"Eli, you're not sick, there's nothing wrong with you that I've found. Although you are pregnant."

"But...I can't be. I mean, Arthur always uses condoms, and..." She paused, trying to process what Dr. Benton was saying. "You can't get pregnant if you're in menopause, so I'm not pregnant."

"You're not in menopause. You're pregnant. Some of those missed periods were because you're going to have a baby, not because of menopause. You're going to have a baby in around six or seven months. Somewhere around May or June would be my guess. We'll have to do some tests to be sure."

"But—"

"Listen, Eli, I've been your doctor for a long time, and I know this comes as a shock. Why don't you go home, take some time and process it all, then come see me again next week and we'll talk? We'll do a few more tests. I want to do a sonogram so we'll have a more accurate idea of your due date since you have been experiencing erratic cycles."

"But—"

"And here." He reached into his pocket and handed her a prescription. "Prenatal, prescription vitamins. Get it filled and start taking one a day."

"But—"

He patted her hand. "It's going to be all right."

Eli went into a type of brain-fogged automatic pilot. That was the only way to explain how she managed to dress and check in with the receptionist. She agreed to the first appointment that was offered without consulting her calendar, bundled into her jacket, and made her way to her car—her brand-new MINI Cooper. A more nonbaby car couldn't be found. She drove a MINI, so there was no way she was pregnant.

The fog started to clear.

Dr. Benton, bless his heart, was wrong. That was the only explanation. She'd seen one of those news shows about doctors and their inaccurate tests. That's what this was. The test was faulty.

Or, since Dr. Benton was getting on in age and probably needed reading glasses, he'd misread the results.

Either way, he was wrong. She was not pregnant.

With a newly found, albeit fuzzy, plan, Eli put her foot to the floor and hurried to her neighborhood pharmacy. While she waited for them to fill the prescription that she probably wouldn't need, she grabbed a basket, then walked up and down the aisles until she found the pregnancy test section.

Six.

There were six different brands of pregnancy tests.

She read the boxes. Digital tests. Plus or minus tests. One box had three individual tests in it…for people who thought they were pregnant frequently? There was no way she would want to go through this sinking feeling more than once.

She studied the boxes. All claimed to be ninety-nine percent accurate.

She took the first box and threw it in her basket.

Just to be on the safe side, she grabbed a second brand and added it.

She started down the aisle. Surely, the tests would prove Dr. Benton was wrong.

But what if they were faulty as well?

She turned back and hurried to the display. She put one of each brand of test in her basket.

There. She'd take all of these and when all six told her she wasn't pregnant, she'd call Dr. Benton and insist he either check the expiration dates on his tests at the office, or that he make an appointment for an eye exam.

Maybe both.

He was going to be embarrassed, she was sure. But she'd laugh it off, and make certain he understood she didn't blame him.

Yes, tell him no harm, no foul.

By the time she got home she was feeling a surreal sense of calm. Everything would be fine once she peed on the six small wands. All of them promised results in three to five minutes.

She glanced at the clock. Dr. Benton would probably still be at his office. She'd call him right away so he could figure out what the problem was…faulty test or aging eyes.

She hurried into the bathroom and discovered peeing on sticks was infinitely easier than peeing in a cup.

She lined them all up on the counter and left, determined not to watch them. She didn't need to. She knew what they were going to show—she wasn't pregnant.

She stood outside the bathroom door, trying to decide what to do while she waited. Aimlessly, she went down the hall and thumbed through her mail that she'd set on the antique washstand she'd found last summer on her New England vacation with Arthur. They'd meandered with no real destination in mind, stopping in small towns and villages along the way.

She ran a finger over the stand, and couldn't help it if her sleeve slipped up, exposing her watch. She didn't mean to check the time and was disappointed to discover that only one minute had passed.

She walked through the house, feeling slightly removed—as if she were a visitor seeing it for the first time. She remembered every item, its history and any sentiment it carried.

Everything was orderly in her tiny, perfect-for-one-person, but not-for-a-baby house. There was her bedroom, with the froufrou pillows on the bed. Arthur hated them and felt that the few seconds she spent putting them in place every day were wasted time. It probably added up to an hour or more a year, he'd told her. Arthur was a big fan of time management, and try as she might, she couldn't seem to convince him that time spent on aesthetics wasn't wasted at all. She liked how the pillows looked on the bed, how the entire room's decor came together. That was worth an hour of her year.

She peeked in her equally neat and appealing office. She'd spent three weekends stripping, then refinishing the oak floor. She'd used a high gloss on them and they truly shone. The deep red walls, the pulled back curtains… her office was an oasis.

This time she didn't try to convince herself that glancing at her watch was an accident.

Two minutes to go.

She went to the kitchen, hoping she'd left a glass or plate in the sink, something she could rinse, but there was nothing.

Her house was too small, too settled for a baby.

She couldn't be pregnant because she'd built a single person's home.

She glanced at her watch again.

Finally knowing beyond any doubt just how Marie Antoinette had felt as she marched toward the chopping block, Eli opened the bathroom door, then one by one picked up the wands.

Pregnant.

Pregnant.

Pregnant.

Pregnant.

Pregnant.

Her hands trembled as she picked up the

last one. One little stick of hope, which was the only branch she had left to hang on to.

Pregnant.

Shit.

Eli wasn't sure how long she sat on the bathroom floor staring at that last stick. It was long enough for the realization to begin to penetrate, long enough that the ramifications of that stick, along with the other five, hit home.

She was pregnant.

Her feet were numb and tingling. One of the changes she'd noticed since hitting her forties was that she could only kneel for so long before all the blood stopped pumping into her legs.

She was well beyond her blood pumping limit.

And she was pregnant.

She wasn't sure what to do. Who to turn to.

She wanted to cry, but had preached to her girls that news of a baby should never be greeted with tears. She'd had so many young moms in her office, crying their eyes out. She understood their feelings, but it struck her as a very sad way to welcome a child into existence, so she wasn't going to cry.

But if she wasn't going to cry, that left her nothing to do with the huge lump that was sitting squarely in the center of her throat.

What to do?

Call Tucker.

She made her wobbly feet walk into the living room and dialed her friend's number. "Could you come over? I need you." She'd known that would be all it took.

Tucker didn't ask any questions, didn't hesitate. "On my way," she replied. That was like her friend. Tucker never expected anything from anyone, but gave unhesitantly to everyone.

Angelina Tucker was Eli's inspiration for starting the teen parenting program. Sixteen years ago, Tucker had been a senior and Eli had been a teacher in the home-ec department for five years. That's what they'd called it then. Now, it was family and consumer sciences.

When Tucker had found out she was pregnant, she'd come to Eli for help, and Eli had discovered how very few options and avenues there were for the young girl. She'd fought for Tucker and had become her advocate. The following year she began to put together a program for the entire district.

Tucker had come into her first classes and

talked about her experiences as a teen mother. Eli had used her as a peer role model for her girls.

As they worked together, something shifted, and Tucker had become a friend. A good friend. Eventually, a best friend.

Eli was even little Bart's godmother.

Okay, Bart wasn't all that little anymore. But Tucker was just the same, hard on the outside, a pushover on the inside.

Tucker would know what to do.

Eli went to the living room and just sat on the couch and waited. When Tucker came, everything would be fine. She clung to that thought.

Tucker didn't knock, but burst into the house fifteen minutes later. There was no prelude, no opening line. She just asked, "What happened?" Concerned lines were etched on her face and she ran her fingers through her short, curly brown hair, which made it look more wild than it usually did.

"I'm pregnant."

Eli had never seen anything stop Tucker in her tracks, but this did.

Tucker plopped down next to Eli on the couch and was quiet a moment.

Then, as if some reserve energy source

engaged, she turned to Eli and smiled. "Okay. If anyone can deal with this, it's you. You know all your options. You've got your education, a good job, a nice house…good friends." There was a firm certainty in Tucker's voice that worked as a balm on some of the raging emotions that roiled through Eli.

"Oh, and you've got Arthur," Tucker added as an afterthought.

"Yeah." Eli realized that when the news had finally sank in her first thought was to call her friend, not Arthur. She didn't want to analyze what that meant. There were too many other things she needed to concentrate on. "I'm a few months along. I thought it was menopause."

Tucker smiled. "Surprise."

Despite her worries, Eli managed a weak smile of her own. "Yeah."

"I remember when I found out about Bart, I was sort of stunned. I went and talked to this very wise teacher and she asked, 'What are you feeling'? She made me dig through all that junk and really pick the emotions apart. So, I'll ask you, what are you feeling?"

Eli tried to sort through the swirling vortex of feelings that were overwhelming her. She grabbed at one. "Terrified. I mean, I'm forty-four. Once upon a time I wanted kids, but I never met the right man, it was never the right time. Years ago I decided that it wasn't meant to be. I have hundreds of kids as in my students. That's enough. I've organized my life in a childless sort of way. I can't have a baby."

"Well, then…" Tucker let the words hang there.

Eli shook her head, surprised at the fierceness of her reaction to Tucker's unspoken suggestion. "No. That's not an option for me. I mean, I just can't."

"Fine, then that's progress. You've made a major decision…you're having this baby. And you're terrified, you didn't expect to have a child. What else are you feeling?"

Eli waded through the mishmash of her emotions. "Foolish. I mean, I work with pregnant mothers for a living, and I didn't realize I was pregnant? That's sad. But in my defense, we used protection every time, and I'm old. Practically ready for menopause."

"Terrified. Foolish. Old. What else?" Tuck pressed.

"Apprehensive. I have to tell my parents before they leave for their winter in Florida… and Arthur, of course."

"I remember how much fun telling my

dad was. But lucky for me, I had this great teacher go with me. Lucky for you, you have a friend who's here if you need back-up with your parents."

Eli noticed that Tucker didn't offer to come tell Arthur with her. She laughed. "What about when I tell Arthur?"

"I'd just antagonize him by—oh, I don't know—breathing or something."

"And he'd reciprocate. It's fine. I'll take that one on my own." The fact that her boy-friend and her best friend didn't get along made things difficult. Eli had learned to com-partmentalize her life. Tucker and the rest of her friends, her school life, on one side, and Arthur on the other.

"What else?" Tucker asked.

Eli pulled her thoughts from Arthur and went back to the question at hand. What else was she feeling? She searched, and finally caught on a weak, almost whisper of a feeling. "Under all of that, there's a bit of ex-citement. I mean, I never thought it would happen, that I'd have a baby. Truth of the matter is, I'm going to be a mother. Sure there's a lot to figure out, and it's not conve-nient, but then it was that way with Bart and look at how tight the two of you are."

She stopped a second and added, "I've never asked before, but do you regret it? I mean, I know you love him, but do you ever regret everything you had to go through?"

"There are parts that I wouldn't want to relive, but he's such an amazing kid, I can't imagine what my life would be without him. I don't regret a minute of it. Having him led me to where I am. I have a kid I adore, a job I love and a friend I might never have found if I hadn't shown up in her classroom that day asking for help."

Eli couldn't think of anything to say to that.

Tucker didn't seem to mind. After another silent moment passed, she asked, "You want me to call Bart and tell him that he's on his own for dinner? We'll order a pizza and pig out. You can do that guilt-free now that you're eating for two."

Eli laughed, which she knew had been Tucker's intent. "No. I'm fine now. Well, not quite fine, but on my way to it. I need some time alone to sort it all out. Though it's so good to know that you're just a phone call away. You really helped settle me down."

"I'm no expert. I mean, I just paint stuff for a living—"

Tucker always underplayed her talent, and Eli felt obliged to interrupt and correct her description of her job. "A graphic artist. What you do is art, Tuck."

Tucker shrugged and stood. "Doesn't matter what you call it, I'm a simple woman who has to say something before I leave. It's something no one but you ever said to me. Congratulations, Eli. This baby will change your life. And though you don't see it now, it will change your life for the better. I just know it."

Tucker leaned down and, in an uncharacteristic display of affection, hugged Eli. "No matter what, you just remember that you're not alone."

She waved and hurried out.

Eli knew that Tucker was embarrassed at her actions. She wasn't a hugger, wasn't prone to inspirational speeches. However, this one hit the mark.

This baby was going to change Eli's life.

She could only hope Tucker was right and that it was for the better.

Eli spent the rest of the evening wandering from one room of the house to another, thinking. What was Arthur going to say? Would he be excited? And her parents? Were they going to be disappointed in her?

She knew she was well past the age where she needed her parents' approval, but that didn't stop her from enjoying it. It didn't stop the sting of imagining she'd let them down.

She went into the bathroom and cleared away the remnants of her momentary insanity. She was going to have a baby, and no amount of testing was going to change that.

Bathroom cleaned, she stood in the hall not sure what to do or where to go.

Finally, she went to her room, threw the decorative pillows onto the floor, rather than stacking them neatly on the chest, and climbed into bed fully clothed. She burrowed under the covers and willed sleep to come and take her away from all her worries.

When it didn't, she tugged up on her shirt and exposed her stomach. Gently she ran her hands over it. Not *it,* her baby.

Her baby was there.

She was going to be a mother.

She just let the enormity of that thought sit there, blocking all her other considerations.

She had six sticks and a doctor's test to prove that in a very short time she was going to be someone's mom.

She was going to change diapers and breastfeed. She was going to get up in the middle of the night and deal with teething.

Somewhere down the line she'd have to cope with a first day of school, book reports and science fairs. Even first loves.

She was going to be a mother.

And someday in about eighteen years, this baby would graduate from school and go away to college. Maybe stay away, too, if the right job came along.

Her baby would someday leave her.

A new emotion swamped her. Loneliness. She'd miss this baby she'd only just found out about. Her child would eventually find their own way, build their own life, one that didn't center around her. She'd be peripheral at best.

She rested her hand on her stomach and promised herself that when that day came she'd let go. Until then, she'd hold on tight and try to enjoy every minute.

Enjoy.

Yes, under the myriad emotions that had assaulted her since she got the news was excitement. Now joined by the promise of enjoyment. She was going to enjoy being a mother.

At least she thought she would.

Oh, there was still panic, terror, but she clung to the more positive emotions.

She was going to be a mother.

CHAPTER TWO

"Discovering you're pregnant means things will change, but different isn't always worse…"
—*Pregnancy, Childbirth and Parenting for Teens,* by Mary Jeanne Lorei

"MS. CARTWRIGHT, ARE YOU OKAY?" Ariel asked the next day after class.

Eli had thought she was doing an admirable job hiding her sleepless night and inner turmoil, but obviously, she was wrong.

She redoubled her efforts and pasted her best I'm-okay smile on and nodded. "I'm fine, thanks."

"I promised we'd finish our discussion. I wrote the note and will give it to Mrs. Brown this afternoon."

"Good. That's a great start." At the word *start,* the girl's smile faded.

"You said we'd talk about what else I need

to do? I've been trying to think of what else could fix this, but other than taking an F on that test, I can't think of anything."

"Actually, Mrs. Brown and I talked about that. Rather than fail you, we've agreed that you'll retake the test. And then she'll deduct ten percent from whatever you get as a penalty."

"Thank you. I assumed I'd get an F and that would drop my GPA."

Eli smiled. Despite her own mind, she'd given Ariel's situation some thought. To be honest, thinking about Ariel was so much easier than thinking about herself.

"I have an idea," she told the girl. "After my meeting this afternoon, I'll fill you in."

Ariel looked nervous.

"It's not bad," Eli assured her. "As a matter of fact, I think this might work out to be a very, very good thing for you."

Suddenly Ariel's expression changed to a look children had worn on Christmas Eve for centuries. "Ms. Cartwright, do you want to give me a hint?"

Eli chuckled. "No. But come see me after school."

"You're sure?"

"Go. I don't want you being late for your next class."

When Ariel left, Eli went back to crunching figures and making sure her facts were in order. She wished she could find the enthusiasm for this meeting she once had. Today everything felt muted. Dampened. As if she were viewing the world through cotton gauze.

She kept eying the clock.

Finally.

Lunchtime.

She stood and smoothed her skirt, then without realizing it, her hand brushed her stomach, as if to make sure her baby was all right.

Baby.

Her baby.

It still felt so unreal. Part of her would have liked to deny the reality, but those six little sticks wouldn't allow her to.

She had a standing dinner date with Arthur on Friday nights. So tomorrow, she'd tell him. She could almost imagine stoic, dependable Arthur's reaction. He would probably be as shocked as she was, but he'd be supportive. He'd understand her mixed emotions over this unplanned, life-altering event.

Together, they'd work it out.

Right now, she needed to put all that aside and get going or she'd be late for this meeting.

She stopped at the main office and checked out with the school secretary. "Doris, I'm not sure when I'll be back. If anyone needs me, I'll have my cell. Marion's covering my one o'clock class."

"Good luck. I know how important this meeting is to you, to the new program."

"Thanks. I'm pretty sure he's on board. Today we're supposed to finalize everything and decide on our test-student."

"You'll do fine. Just give me a holler when you get back in." Doris had been with the school longer than Eli. Longer than most of the staff. She was an icon. She ran the main office with a fluid efficiency and had an aura of everyone's favorite grandmother about her.

Her confidence in Eli's ability to make this work helped bolster her own flagging belief in herself.

She drove across Whedon, wishing that this meeting was in an office. She felt at home in that setting or in a classroom. But a local restaurant had sounded convenient when she'd agreed to it. Instead she now worried the location would detract from the business Zac needed to accomplish.

"Eli," he called, waving.

Despite the craziness since her doctor's appointment, seeing him made her smile. There was something engaging about Zac Keller. He was a nice-looking man who was defined by what he wasn't. He wasn't tall, wasn't short—maybe about five-ten. He wasn't fat, wasn't skinny, wasn't a bodybuilder, wasn't scrawny. He had average brown hair and a medium complexion.

But once someone met Zac, he stood out. Maybe it was the devilish look in his brown eyes—a look that said life was a joy and there was always mischief to be made.

"Hi," she said as she took the seat across from him.

His smile faded as he studied her a moment. "What's wrong?"

"Wrong?" she repeated dumbly.

"Wrong. Something's wrong."

First Ariel, now Zac.

Eli tried to school her expression and concentrate on the task at hand.

She passed a file to him. "Not wrong, exactly. Although…"

She jerked her head toward the file. He took the hint and opened it. "Ariel Mayor?"

She nodded. "I'd like her to be the first student we enroll in the program."

"And this troubles you because…?"

"She's having a hard time of it. To be honest, she's the type of student the Community Action Teen-Parent Apprentice Project was designed for. She's a senior who's always been a straight A student, popular with her peers and teachers. If you'd asked me, asked any of her teachers, we'd have told you that she was one of those kids who are blessed. Yet when her parents found out she was pregnant, at the beginning of the school year, they kicked her out. I got involved and learned that Ariel's home life was less than blessed. She's staying at an aunt's, working at a nearby restaurant, going to school, and other than one small incident, she's done a good job balancing everything. She's college material."

Eli paused, needing to make this absolutely pitch perfect. Working for Zac instead, in the CATA Project, could make such a difference for this girl. "Zac, I think it would be a shame if she didn't go to college because of the baby. She deserves to have the life she planned."

"With a baby in the picture, even if she goes to college, it won't be exactly as she planned," he pointed out.

"No, not exactly. But what in life ever goes exactly how we plan?" Eli might have said those same words a few days ago. And she'd have believed them. But now, they rang truer.

As if he'd read her mind, Zac asked, "You didn't plan to be here?"

Here? Pregnant? She almost snorted, but then Zac added, "Helping teen parents?"

Oh. Yes, of course, that's what he meant. "No. Truth is, I never planned this to be my life's work. I stumbled into it when a girl in my class became pregnant and asked for my help. When I looked for services in the district, I realized there was nothing."

"So you helped her yourself?"

She laughed. "Don't make it sound all noble. I liked her. Still do. Over the years, she's become my best friend. I'm surrogate aunt to her son."

"When the school district didn't help, you stepped up and did it yourself. That's not a question. I know you, Eli. You couldn't stand by and not try to do something positive."

He'd said things like that before and as always it made her uncomfortable. Not in a stalker sort of way, but this man saw her in a way no one else did, not even herself.

"Don't glamorize it. I was in the right place at the right time and simply did what needed to be done. Anyone could have done it."

He snorted. "I don't want to argue with you, but you're wrong." As if sensing she was about to dispute it more, he picked the file back up. "So, Ariel's going to be our guinea pig?"

"If you agree. I noted in the file that she's never been in trouble, except for the recent incident. And I don't believe that would have happened if she hadn't been stretched so thin. That's where you come in. No more late hours, time for homework…support."

"Fine." He tapped the file on the table. "Ariel Mayor is our inaugural student in the CATA Project." He raised his water glass. "To many years of a successful partnership between us."

She clinked her glass against his.

"Now, let's order lunch and get down to the nitty-gritty of how we're going to make this work."

Eli had so much to do. So many things to think about. She knew she should excuse herself, instead, she found herself saying,

"So, did you find out what the special is today?"

After they ordered, Zac asked, "So what else is new with you?"

If only she could tell him, but she wasn't about to when her parents and Arthur still didn't know, so she simply said, "Not much. You?"

"Well, I was in some little Podunk town and I…"

Eli listened to Zac's story and soon forgot all her worries. Like Tucker had said, they'd be there tomorrow. Or rather tomorrow night when she went to see Arthur.

THE HOUR FLEW BY TOO FAST in Zac Keller's opinion.

He always enjoyed Eli Cartwright's company. There was something about her that touched him. Her enthusiasm for her work. The girls she taught were more than a job. He could see it in her expression as she talked about them. And this Ariel Mayor he'd just hired was obviously a favorite.

Eli'd talked of her boyfriend in the past, which was the only reason Zac hadn't long since asked her out. Even if he couldn't date her though, he could enjoy her company.

"Why don't we meet on Saturday morning? I'll treat you to coffee at Tim Horton's—the one next to Keller's Market. Then we can both go over and meet your Ariel?"

"You want me there?"

"Not for future student hires, but for this first one, I thought it might be a good idea if we both followed Ariel's progress closely. We can see what works, and where there's room for improvement. I'd like CATA to become one of Keller's pet projects, so I think it's best to really concentrate on this first student and make sure everything runs smoothly."

"I appreciate it, Zac. I don't know if you understand what this program could offer to our girls."

"I think I understand, at least as much as I can."

Eli glanced at her watch. "I better get going."

"See you Saturday, around nine, then? Tell Ariel to meet us at the market at nine-thirty?"

"Sounds good."

She stood, and he immediately followed suit. She thrust out her hand and they shook. "Thanks again, Zac."

"No problem. And Eli, I know we're just business associates, but if you want to talk about whatever's wrong, I'm here." Before she could deny there was anything wrong, or laugh at the idea of her needing his help, he took the bill and headed for the register.

She followed him, and handed him a ten, then, before he could protest, dashed out. "See you Saturday," she called over her shoulder.

Zac knew he should return to his office at the market, but he felt an uncharacteristic urge not to. So instead, he drove in the opposite direction toward his parents' house, under the guise of talking to his father about the business.

The house on East Street was a rambling building. The original one-story heart of the house was built in 1898, and generations of owners had added a room here and a room there, leaving a building with unusual lines. His parents had purchased it forty years ago, a month before they married, determined to fill the seven bedrooms with children.

They'd waited.

And waited.

After waiting ten years, with only their master bedroom in use, they'd decided on adoption.

Zac was their first child.

He was only five but he could still remember his social worker, Mrs. Bowler, pulling up in front of the house, with its flower beds and porch swing. He'd been sure that there was a mistake, that the man and woman waiting on the steps had wanted one of the other boys in the group home. But then the woman had knelt down, held her arms wide and said, "Welcome home, Zac." A feeling of disbelief and hope had filled him.

It was the same feeling he got whenever he pulled in to the driveway.

He hurried into the house. "Mom? Dad?"

He was already almost in the kitchen when his mother called, "In here, Zac."

Deborah Keller was a petite, well-rounded woman, with salt-and-pepper hair she'd pulled loosely into some kind of bun thing, and a smile that lit up the room. She swept Zac into a hug.

He sniffed the sweet scented air. "Cookies? Cake?"

"Gingerbread, *tateleh.*" She glanced at the clock. "If you wait about ten minutes, you should be able to sample a piece and let me know if the new recipe is as good as the old one."

"You could probably twist my arm into

staying." He pulled a stool up to the counter. "Cessy home yet?"

"Not for a while. If you have time to wait, I know she'd be thrilled to see you. The house is just too quiet since Layla went to college." His mom grinned at him. "Of course, if our older children started marrying and gave me grandchildren…" She let the sentence hang there, since he'd heard the entire spiel more than once.

"Just so happens I had lunch with a lovely woman."

"You did?"

His mom seemed so happy, he felt guilty about misleading her, and added, "Of course, she's got a boyfriend."

"A serious boyfriend, or just some man she's seeing?"

He laughed. "I was only kidding, Mom. It's serious between them, I guess. They've been together now for five years." He'd collected a lot of Eli Cartwright trivia since he met her a few months back.

"Five years, and they're still dating?" She shook her head. "That's not serious, that's going with the status quo. Why, your father saw me at the fair—"

"And knew I'd met the woman I was going

to marry right then and there," Abe Keller finished the sentence as he walked into the kitchen. He was a big man. He had a Grizzly Adams look about him. A bit wild. His hair was always unkempt and he went days on end without shaving now that he'd retired from Keller's and left the business to Zac.

Zac watched his father walk over and simply place his hand on his mother's shoulder—he'd noticed years ago that whenever they saw each other it was as if they needed to touch, to reconnect.

His hand still in place, his father continued the story. "And three months later, I married her. So, why are we trotting out that old story? Did your mom want to set you up?"

"No. I don't set my children up. I trust them to find their own dates. Zac was just telling me he had lunch with a woman who's been dating a man for five years. That's not a relationship."

"Now, Deborah, we can't measure other's relationships by ours. If it works for them." His father shrugged.

But Zac could, and always would, measure every relationship against his parents'. This is what he wanted. Someone who needed to touch him, even if they'd only been a room away for a few minutes.

"She's not the one for me, Mom," Zac admitted with regret. "But when I find a woman as good as you are, one who's not dating someone else, you can be sure I'll whisk her off her feet as quickly as I can."

The timer buzzed. His mom busied herself with the gingerbread and his father took the stool opposite him. "So, if you didn't come to get set up…?"

"Thought I'd fill you in on the store."

The next forty-five minutes passed quickly as he and his dad talked business and his mother bustled around the kitchen starting dinner.

Then he heard someone enter before any of them saw her. "Zac." Cessy ran into the room at full speed, still wearing her coat and bookbag, and threw herself full force at him, trusting he'd catch her.

He stood and did. He hugged his fifteen-year-old sister, Cessy, with her mass of curly brown hair, and her honey-toned skin. She backed up. He was five-ten, and she was almost as tall as he was now. "Stop growing, already, would you?"

"Poor little Zac, intimidated by a tall, strong woman?" she teased.

"If I see one of those, I'll let you know if I'm intimidated."

"Hey, you coming to my game on Sunday afternoon?"

"Wouldn't miss it."

"Good, 'cause May, Dom and Layla aren't coming in from Pittsburgh. And Seth—" Cessy stopped short and looked at him. No one talked about Seth, who couldn't forgive their parents for not being enthusiastic about him marrying Allie right out of high school. They'd loved her. The whole family loved her. Still, their parents had wanted them to wait, but Seth and Allie wouldn't. When she got pregnant, they'd started to mend the rift, but when Allie died... Zac wasn't sure what it would take for his parents and Seth to fix their relationship. Seth hadn't cut them off completely, but he'd erected a wall that their parents couldn't breach.

He knew Cessy was thinking the same thing as she glanced at their mother, and added, "So, it'll be you, Mom and Dad cheering me on."

"I'm pretty sure your brother can make

enough noise that you'll never notice the rest are missing," his mom said.

Zac looked at Cessy's face and knew she'd notice. Cessy, more than the rest of them, needed her family around. Zac would rearrange his Sunday. He'd call Dom and May. Granted, they were in their mid-twenties, and busy with their own lives, but if he told them Cessy wanted them at the game, they'd find a way to be there. Layla would fuss about school work, but if Dom or May did the driving, she'd have a little less than two hours in the car each way to study.

And Seth? Well, he'd try. That's all he could do.

Seth had never gotten over his parents not supporting his marriage to Allie, and since her death, he'd been ever more distant. But for Cessy, he might show up.

Zac would do all he could to get his whole family to the game because it was obviously important to Cessy.

That's what family did—supported each other when it was important.

And the Kellers knew that better than most.

FRIDAY PASSED QUICKLY.

Eli set things up with Ariel for Saturday

morning. She smiled as she remembered the girl's excitement about the job. But that smile quickly faded as the reality of talking to Arthur that night hit her for the umpteenth time.

Eli had never thought of herself as a coward, but right now, she wanted nothing more than to call and cancel her date with Arthur.

Instead, she called Tucker, hoping her friend would tell her to suck it up and just get on with it. That was Tucker's normal attitude. Face whatever scared you. And yet ever since she'd told Tucker she was pregnant, her friend had continually surprised her. Instead of giving her a kick in the butt, she assured Eli that avoiding Arthur wasn't cowardly at all, that it would give Eli time to get her feet back on solid ground.

Eli had used similar phrases to girls entering the program. She'd meant them to be as comforting as she was sure Tucker intended hers to be, but until now Eli'd never realized how hollow they sounded.

She knew her feet weren't going to be on solid ground or anywhere other than limbo until she talked to Arthur and her parents. She wasn't sure how long it was going to take her to adjust to the turn her life had taken, and she couldn't wait any longer. She was pregnant and Arthur deserved to know he was going to be a father.

She clutched the bags with the Chinese takeout as she got out of the car. She'd decided a private dinner was better than a public one for this news.

She stood outside his Brent Hollow condo. The development was for people over fifty. No one younger than that could buy a home here. And no children were permitted.

She was going to have to give up her MINI Cooper and buy a more sensible car and she hated the thought, but she was pretty sure Arthur was going to hate giving up his condo more.

She rang the doorbell and part of her wanted to bolt before he came to the door, but she held her ground.

Arthur opened the door. "Hi, honey." He kissed her cheek lightly.

He'd given her a key two years into the relationship. She'd felt it necessary to reciprocate. Neither of them used the keys often, though. They were still on doorbell-ringing status.

"Come in." He took one of the bags. "How's the pilot program going?"

He led her into the living room and set the

bag on the table. They'd shared many meals here, sitting on the floor, in front of a fire during the colder months. He already had the wine open, two glasses waiting.

She sat down across from him, the familiar scene feeling comfortable. "Eli?"

She realized he'd asked about CATA.

"It's going well. Zac's agreed to my suggestion for our first student."

Arthur nodded absently. He didn't ask anything else about the program.

"So how was your week?" she asked, stalling, needing to catch her breath and find a way to gently break the news to him.

Arthur poured their wine, and Eli took up the glass and raised it to her lips, before it occurred to her that she couldn't drink it. She set the glass down and tried to gather her wits as she listened to Arthur go on about the students in his class as he dished up his dinner.

He didn't seem to notice she didn't follow suit.

"Arthur—" She got as far as his name and couldn't think of a way to finish the sentence.

I'm knocked up.

Knock, knock, guess who's knocked up?

What are your plans six or seven months from now?

You know the tour of Europe we've been talking about? What about a tour of local hospital maternity wards instead?

Arthur, I love you and we're going to have a baby.

Hey, Arthur, I'm pregnant. And do you know what irony is? I teach girls who experience unplanned pregnancies, and here I am. I wonder if I can write it off as educational expenses?

"Elinore, are you listening to me?"

She gritted her teeth at the use of her given name. Elinore was a name for someone older, more mature than she was. She was going to have a baby, for goodness sakes, she couldn't be an Elinore yet.

She'd always hated it when he called her that, but today it grated more than it usually did.

"Eli," she snapped.

His fork full of General Tso's chicken froze midway between the plate and his mouth. "What is wrong?"

"I could give you a list, a long, long list of things, but topping it would be the fact I'm pregnant."

Arthur dropped the fork, and the bright red sauce splashed onto his shirt, but he didn't make a move to clean it off. He didn't say a word, but the wave of paleness that moved from the top of his head downward said it all.

Great. Just great. That was slick. What a gentle breaking of unexpected news.

Eli didn't say anything for a few minutes, letting him adjust to the shock.

When a bit of color seemed to seep back into his face, she said, "I know we didn't plan this. It's unexpected. When the doctor told me I didn't believe him. I thought I was entering menopause. I went to the pharmacy and bought one of each brand of pregnancy test there was and the results were all the same. I'm pregnant."

She waited for him to smile at her reaction. Still nothing.

"I go for a second visit on Monday to have a sonogram, but the doctor thinks I'm either entering, or barely into my second trimester."

"Is it mine?"

Of all the responses she'd imagined, this hadn't even made the list of possibilities. "Is it yours?"

He nodded.

"Of course it's yours. I didn't cheat on you."

"I wish you would have." Arthur gave his head a small shake. "I can't have a baby. *We* can't have a… We talked about this up front. I'm almost ready to retire, and you have a busy and satisfying career. We have plans. I want to write my book, we're going to travel. We can't have this…"

"Baby, Arthur. It's a baby. Our baby. I know we didn't plan it, but it's here, a reality we're going to have to cope with. It means adjusting some of our plans, but we can make it work."

He frowned. "Don't you see? I don't want to make it work. And there's nothing to say we have to. That you have to go through with the pregnancy."

Her hand immediately moved to her stomach, as if to protect their baby from the harshness of his suggestion. "Arthur, that's not an option."

"It is. I'd go with you, support you through the whole thing."

"I know it's a surprise, and I wouldn't condemn someone for making that kind of decision, but it's not for me. I couldn't terminate this pregnancy."

"And I can't be a father."

"Oh." Eli didn't know what to say to that. She'd expected him to be as taken aback at the news as she was, but she'd also expected him to hug her, to say he'd be there for her, that everything would be all right.

She hadn't realized how much she'd been counting on that.

"Arthur, we'll talk to someone and find a way to work this out."

He shook his head and his shaggy brown hair tumbled over his eyes. Normally, she'd reach over and push it back into place, but tonight she simply gripped her hands on her lap. "What do you suggest then?"

"If you go through with this, I can't be a part of it. I want nothing to do with the baby. Nothing."

There was a finality in his tone that cut straight through her. It was almost a physical pain. But Eli wouldn't give in to it. She sat up straighter. "Fine. You'll have to see a lawyer, have him draw up papers terminating your parental rights because I won't have you playing on-again, off-again father."

"That's not a worry because I have no wish to be anyone's father. I'll see my lawyer, have the papers drawn up. I'll open a college fund for the baby, in lieu of paying child support, if that works for you."

She wanted to tell him to keep his money,

that they wouldn't need it, but a practical side of her knew that someday the baby would need substantial financial help with college.

"Fine." Somehow she found the strength to stand. "Goodbye, Arthur."

He stood as well, and moved next to her. "I didn't want things to end like this."

"I didn't, either." She'd barely begun to adjust to the idea of a baby, but when she'd pictured what it would be like to be a mother, she'd imagined Arthur by her side, learning to be a father. It was another future she'd have to let go of.

"Keep in touch." He moved toward her, as if to hug her.

Eli took a quick step backward. She didn't want to touch Arthur Stone. Didn't want the pity she saw in his eyes. She shook her head. "I don't think so. If we're going to make a break, let's make it clean. Call me when you've got the papers, and that will be the last you'll hear from me."

"Elinore—"

"Eli." And with all the dignity she could muster, she held her head high and walked out of Arthur's condo.

She got into her MINI and sat a moment,

her hand pressed to her stomach. "Looks like it's just you and me, kid," she whispered.

Despite what she'd said to Arthur, she wasn't sure she could handle this. Wasn't sure at all. Unlike Arthur, though, she didn't have a choice. She couldn't walk away.

She snapped her seat belt into place, put her key in the ignition, then the car in Drive and left.

Left Arthur, and left the life she'd thought she'd have.

For the first time in years, Eli Cartwright was driving without a map. It was disconcerting. It was terrifying.

Underneath all that, there was also just the tiniest bit of exhilaration. There was suddenly a potential that hadn't been there before.

Rather than driving home, Eli headed toward Tucker's, knowing her friend would be a hundred percent on her side.

But half an hour later, when Eli finished telling Tucker about her meeting with Arthur, her friend's reaction was far more vehement than Eli had imagined.

Tucker paced back and forth in her living room. "Penis. Goat-boffing, self-important eunuch of a man."

"Tucker, sit down next to me." Eli patted the empty couch cushion. "I feel I have to point out Arthur couldn't boff goats if he was a eunuch."

Tucker didn't stop pacing. Instead, she kicked the ottoman. "He could try. I hope—"

"Stop right there," Eli warned. "You're not going to tempt the fates by wishing any plagues—"

"I was going for some penis-eating venereal disease, but a plague would work."

Eli laughed. Tucker's reaction was almost a balm to her wounded pride. "How could I have wasted five years of my life on someone who could desert a child?"

Tucker finally sat, but remained resolutely silent.

"You tried to tell me, and I appreciate your not saying 'I told you so,' but I'll say it for you—you told me so."

"I never in a million years would have expected him to just walk away from this. Oh, I thought he was a boring, pontificating prig—"

"Prig?"

"I've been reading historical romances again, and it's a good descriptive word. And though I thought it would describe Arthur, I still would never have guessed he'd abandon you. To be honest, I can't imagine him not having opinions—many, many opinions—on how a child of his should be raised."

"Actually, he doesn't want it to be raised. He wanted me to go for an abortion."

"Rat bastard."

Bart stuck his head in the doorway. "Mom, phone. It's a guy, some Tyler Martinez." He spotted Eli and waved. "Hey, Aunt Eli." He ducked back out again.

"Speaking of rat bastards," Tucker murmured more to herself than to Eli. She got up and took the phone.

"Yes?"

She listened and was soon scowling. "Are you crazy? No." And without saying anything further, she hung up.

"Problems with a customer?" Eli asked.

Tucker shook her head and plopped back onto the couch. "Nothing you need to worry about. The way I see it, you've got more than enough on your plate."

"Maybe whatever's going on with you would distract me? And I so need to be distracted."

"Nothing's going on, really. Just a man asking for a date."

Tucker hadn't dated often over the years. Not that she wasn't asked out, but more often than not, she declined. Eli worried about her. Tucker was still young. She should go out and have a good time on occasion. "Is this guy a troll?"

"No. He's gorgeous, actually, in a sleek, magazine-ad way." Tucker's scowl made the idea of a gorgeous man seem less appealing than dental surgery.

"So he's boorish?"

"Not exactly. Despite his prissy way, he gets along great with Dad and the other guys in the garage."

"A prig like Arthur then?" She smiled as she used the word.

Tucker shook her head.

"Married? Twelve kids?"

Another no.

"Okay, so a gorgeous, interesting, unattached man who gets along with your father called to ask you out and you say no why?"

"I say no every time he asks."

"He's asked more than once?" This was the first Eli had heard about this Tyler Martinez, and she couldn't help but wonder if there were other men who'd asked Tucker out that she hadn't mentioned.

"He's asked me out a few times," Tucker admitted.

"What am I missing?"

"Some brain cells if you can't figure it out. I mean, I'm pretty sure his suits are designer—not that I know designer clothes. I mean, there's Jacqueline Smith stuff at Kmart, but otherwise?" She shrugged. "Anyway, I'm pretty sure that's what his stuff is, and he's certainly got money to burn."

Eli shook her head, genuinely confused. "Still not getting it."

"Look at me, do I look like the type of woman a man like that would be interested in?"

Eli did look. Tucker was wearing a holey pair of jeans, some steel-toed work boots and a T-shirt that proudly proclaimed It's NASCAR or Nothin'. The T-shirt was worn thin from too many washings, and hugged Tucker's body in such a way that no man could miss that despite the work clothes, Tucker was all woman. "I don't see why he wouldn't be interested, Tuck. I mean, if I were a man, I'd try to date you."

Her outrageous comment had the desired effect. Tucker laughed. "If you were a man

I'd probably say yes. But he's different. Too different."

"Tucker, this Tyler, or any man, would be all kind of lucky to have a woman like you."

Tucker pulled back, not physically, but emotionally. Eli could talk herself blue in the face, but Tucker would never believe that she was beautiful. It had nothing to do with designer clothes, and everything to do with the kind of woman Tucker was.

And part of what made Tucker Tucker was her complete and annoying stubbornness, which reared its head now. "Let's change the subject back to you. What are you going to do now?"

"I made plans for dinner with my parents tomorrow night. I expect it's going to go about as well, or even worse, than how it went telling Arthur." She loved her parents, saw them at least once a week when they were in town, and talked to them frequently when they wintered in Florida each year. The fact that she would be an unwed mother was not going to impress them. She was forty-four, but obviously the desire to please a parent didn't go away with age. It might even have gotten stronger.

"I think you're wrong. They might not be

happy, but they'll stand by you. I have no doubt of that."

"You're right. It still won't be pretty."

"Maybe you're wrong."

"Yeah, maybe. And maybe the earth is going to start rotating backward, and all the bad guys will suddenly become good guys forever and ever."

She snorted. "And maybe prigs will fly."

Maybe.

But Eli wasn't betting on any of it.

CHAPTER THREE

"Time. It can feel as if you don't have nearly enough time to get everything done. Remember, despite all you need to do, take time to have some fun."

—*Pregnancy, Childbirth and Parenting for Teens,* by Mary Jeanne Lorei

ELI NORMALLY LOVED SATURDAYS. She loved knowing she didn't have to get up and do anything. She loved the idea of leisurely walks, and reading the paper—front to back—over a second cup of coffee. Then possibly doing the crossword puzzle in ink over a third cup.

Today, there was no sense of happiness at the thought as she glanced at the clock. 8:00 a.m.

She didn't have time for the paper before her meeting with Zac, and even if she did, there'd be no coffee. No caffeine for her for the rest of the pregnancy. And probably not while she was breast-feeding, either. If she breast-fed. Would she breast-feed?

Another decision.

One she simply couldn't face.

She had to get together with Zac Keller and Ariel Mayor, then she had to hurry home and clean the house before her parents' visit.

Not that her house was a mess. And she didn't generally clean before her parents came over. But since she was about to break the fact she was pregnant with no father in the picture, she figured the least she could do was tell them in a spotless house.

After all, that wasn't too much to ask, was it?

And why on earth did she let Zac talk her into meeting at Tim Horton's? To smell that wonderful coffee and not be able to have a cup was going to be sheer torture. Okay, she could probably order a decaf, but seriously, if she couldn't drink the real thing, why bother?

She hurried out to the car, pulling her winter coat tighter.

Winter hadn't even officially arrived—heck, autumn was only halfway gone—but she was ready for spring.

The thought stopped her in her tracks. By late spring, she'd have her baby. Right at the end of the school year. She'd be a mother. Her whole life would change.

Sometimes, she'd forget she was pregnant. Then, she'd have one of those moments of awareness.

She *was* pregnant.

She *was* going to be a mother.

She kept repeating the words as she drove to the coffee shop.

There was no denying it. The life she'd planned was gone thanks to this baby. A small spurt of anger surprised her. She didn't blame the baby, but she was mad at the circumstances. Arthur could throw up his hands and walk away. She was stuck. Her body wasn't ever going to be the same. Her life was never going to be the same. It wasn't fair.

It wasn't fair. She couldn't count the number of times girls said those words to her. Her response? Life's not fair. Deal with it.

She realized she'd been parked in front of the coffee shop for…she wasn't sure how long.

Yeah, life's not fair. Deal with it.

Right now she had to deal with Zac Keller.

She hurried inside and scanned the place. She spotted Zac in line and approached him.

A slow smile spread on his face. "You made it."

"We'd agreed, so of course I made it."

"What would you like?" He nodded at the menu.

"A house decaf." She wanted her caffeine. Wanted it desperately. Already, the baby was impacting her life. Her decisions.

"After all our meetings, you switching to decaf just seems wrong."

He was teasing, and Eli knew it, so she smiled. "I'm turning over a new leaf. Actually, a few new leaves." Whether she wanted to or not.

"How does Arthur feel about these changes?"

"Arthur's out of the picture." It was the first time she'd said the words out loud in conversation. It made the fact he was gone seem more real. More permanent.

"We broke up," she added, more for herself than for Zac.

"Oh." Zac paused. "Sorry."

"Our relationship had progressed as far as it could. It was time to make a clean break."

Zac seemed puzzled, and Eli waited for him to ask her more questions, but after a moment, he nodded. They waited in silence for their coffees.

She wondered what he was thinking.

But he didn't give her a clue. After their drinks were in hand, he simply said, "Why don't we take the coffees next door to my office and I can show you the schedule we've put together for Ariel."

"Great."

ZAC AND ELI CONTINUED in silence as they walked to Keller's Market. Other than the first day, they'd never met in his office. He always insisted they meet over a lunch or coffees. It seemed more relaxed, more personal. And that was just what he'd wanted to be with Eli Cartwright.

The news that she'd broken up with her boyfriend meant he was free to get even more up close and personal.

He'd love to ask her out right away, but he knew he should wait and give her some time to recover from the breakup.

How much time did it require?

Hours?

Days?

Not weeks. No, weeks was too long. Some other guy was bound to ask Eli on a date as soon as the news got out that she was available. Zac wasn't going to lose out to some quick-on-the-draw stranger.

Since he knew he had to wait, this once, keeping things all business was probably for the best. That was why he suggested taking their coffees to his office.

"Zac?" Eli said.

He noticed they were standing in his office doorway. "Sorry. Thinking about things I have to do." Mainly asking out Eli. "Have a seat."

He had a copy of Ariel's schedule in his briefcase, but handed her the one on his desk instead. "Here you go."

She reached for it, and for the briefest second, their fingers touched. Zac didn't think of himself as a sentimental sort of man, which is why his awareness of that smallest of touches surprised him. Of course, it shouldn't have. Yet, everything about Eli Cartwright touched him.

"It looks—"

Eli was cut off as Cessy burst into his office. "Z-man, help. I need a ride to—" Cessy stopped short as she caught sight of Eli. "Sorry, Ms. Cartwright. I'm not used to Zac having people in his office this early on a Saturday morning. I'm much better behaved on weekdays. Uh, the principal didn't send you in to talk to Zac about my inability to be quiet in class, did he?"

Eli laughed. "No. I'm not here about you."

Zac knew he should reprimand his irrepressible sister, but she stood there grinning and practically radiating happiness. He couldn't muster up even a small tsk of disapproval.

She ran a hand over her brow. "Phew. I'd rather the principal talk to Mom and Dad any day of the week. They're pushovers. Zac, he's tough."

He laughed. "Yeah, that's why you're coming to me for a ride somewhere, because of my world-renowned toughness?"

"Zac, I say you're tough in front of people so they won't catch on to what a marshmallow you are." She fished in her pocket and pulled out a small thing to twist her wildly curly hair into a ponytail.

"So, where are we riding to?" he asked.

"I was sort of hoping you'd drive me over to Grove City's outlets after I finish my morning shift. They're having a preholiday sale, and I'd really like to go do some early Christmas shopping."

"Mom and Dad said you could go?"

She shook her head. "I'm going to ask after I have everything set up. It makes it harder for them to say no if I have all my bases covered."

He chuckled. "Sure."

"Thanks. See you later, Ms. Cartwright." His sister gave a small wave, then proceeded toward the door.

"Hey, Cessy," Zac called, halting her progress, "don't forget I'm sending down a new employee for you to show the ropes to."

"I won't forget. And I'll have her swinging from the ropes before the morning's over," she promised. "And Zac, don't forget your promise…I'm Cecily out in public." And with that reminder, she ran out of the office.

"So Cecily's your sister? You don't look anything alike."

Zac knew that was an understatement. "We're both adopted. Actually, I'm the oldest of five. We were all adopted, so there's no family resemblance, but maybe that's why we're so tight. Cessy—" remembering his promise, he corrected himself "—pardon me, *Cecily* is fifteen, she's the youngest."

"I should have put the last names together. She's a whirlwind. I don't have her in any classes, but I see her around school and hear her name on the announcements a lot because of sports. It's hard not to know who Cecily Keller is."

"That was a very polite way of saying

Cessy is loud. When she asked if you were here on a mission from the school, it was only because it wouldn't be the first time we'd had reports of Cecily's—" he searched for the appropriate word to describe his sister "—exuberance."

"That's an apt description."

"I was going to use boisterous, but exuberant sounded—"

Cessy interrupted as she burst back through the door, a tall blonde behind her. "Hey, Ariel's here. Ariel, my brother Zac Keller. Zac, this is Ariel." Introductions made, she turned to Ariel. "Go pretend to listen to him—he likes it when employees act as if they hold him in high esteem and appear to hang on his every word."

"Something my little sister doesn't even bother to pretend to do."

Cessy cackled. "Like I'd feed your over-inflated ego, Mr. Keller, sir." She dropped her voice to a stage whisper. "You're making Ariel nervous, Z-man."

"I'm not nervous," Ariel protested, standing straight and squaring her shoulders as if to prove the point.

"Good, 'cause I can assure you, my brother's a pushover. Go listen to his spiel, then I'll show you around." Cessy flew back through the door, shutting it loudly behind her.

Zac turned to Eli. "You're sure you're not here on behalf of the school to talk to me about my sister?"

She grinned. "She's just exuberant. Remember?"

He grinned. "Hi, Ariel. Have a seat."

Eli patted the chair next to her. "Come sit down."

When Ariel was settled, both women looked at him. He didn't want to dive right into business. He wanted to put the girl at ease. "You and Cecily are friends?"

"We know each other, Mr. Keller. The school's small enough that it's hard not to know everyone. But she hangs out with the jocks—" she stopped abruptly and amended "—basketball team, and until recently, I hung out with the cheerleaders."

"Two different circles in high school terms," Eli explained.

"But we get along, Mr. Keller," Ariel added hastily.

"Call me Zac. We're not very formal at Keller's."

He could see the girl was nervous. Eli

must have sensed it, too. She slid the paper she'd been looking at before Cessy's entrance toward Ariel. "Zac was showing me the schedule he drew up for you."

"It's only preliminary. We can fine-tune it as you get comfortable and see what works. And later, when the baby comes, we'll adjust it even more."

Ariel studied the schedule for a minute. "Thanks. This is so much better than the hours at the restaurant."

"Well, if it gets to be too much, say something. I thought we'd start you out on the register. And Ariel, Keller's offers partial scholarships to any of our employees who are going to college. You need a good work record, and at least a B average at school, and we can help defray some of your education costs. Ms. Cartwright has glowing things to say about you, including the fact that you are definitely on the college track."

"Really?" Ariel looked surprised.

He wasn't sure if she was asking *really* about the partial scholarship, or *really* about whether Eli really had glowing things to say about her. He simply answered, "Really."

"I appreciate the opportunity, Mr. Keller. I'll do my best to make you and Ms. Cartwright proud. I've made so many mistakes lately, but I will try to do better."

"Ariel, everyone makes mistakes," Eli assured her. "Life happens. What truly defines us as people is how we handle what life throws at us."

Zac nodded. "Do your best. That's all we ask for here at Keller's. And remember, I'm here if you need anything." He figured that about covered what he needed to say today, so he added, "Why don't you go find Cecily and let her show you around? Tell her to put you on the clock for the tour. And make sure she takes you to Millie, to fill out all the paperwork."

Ariel stood. "Really, Mr. Keller, Ms. Cartwright. Thank you."

Eli reached up, took Ariel's hand and gave it a squeeze. "You're going to do great, Ariel. I'll look for you when I'm getting ready to go."

Just as Ariel left the room, Eli's cell phone rang. She pulled it from her bag, glanced at the number and asked, "Do you mind?"

"No problem."

She got up and stepped outside the office. Moments later she was back.

"Problems?"

"No. My parents called to cancel our

dinner plans. Seems some old neighbors are in town only for the weekend, and they're seeing them." She sat back down with a sigh. "It's a relief, actually."

"You don't get along with your parents?" He knew better than most that not all parents were created equal. He hated the thought of Eli growing up in a bad situation.

"No, I didn't mean it to sound that way," she assured him. "It's nothing like that. I have some news for them, and I don't think they're going to like it, so the reprieve is not a bad thing."

"Do you want to talk about it?" As he said the words, Zac admitted that he wished she would confide in him. She looked so stressed at the thought of whatever she needed to tell her parents. He wanted nothing more than to ease some of that burden.

"Thanks. But I'm not really ready to talk to anyone about it. At least, not yet."

She probably needed to tell them she'd broken up with the boyfriend. Maybe they'd liked him and that's why she was reluctant to tell them. "Hey, if you were going to be with your parents, that means you don't have plans anymore, right?"

She nodded slowly. "Right."

"Why don't you come with us to Grove

City? We could ask Ariel to come as well. From what little you've said, it sounds as if she'd appreciate having some fun. We could all make a day of it."

"I don't know. There are a million and one things I should be doing."

"I'm all for doing what should be done, but sometimes, there's merit in taking a break. And to sweeten the offer, there's a great restaurant right outside the outlet mall. We could grab something to eat and take your mind off your parents."

"Are you sure? I don't want to intrude on your time with your sister."

Zac didn't want to tell her just how sure he was and scare her off. So he settled for, "Of course, I am. I mean, I'm smart enough to want an ally while shopping at an outlet mall with a teen."

She chuckled. "Ah, so asking me was selfish on your part."

Eli's laughter. It was one of the things about her that got to him. She worked with kids who were in such tough straits. He'd seen how she went to the wall for each and every one. And still, despite the fact she dealt with such trying experiences, she still managed to find the joy in things.

"Eli, I can assure you that my asking you was definitely in my own self-interest. Absolutely selfish."

"Glad to know you have a flaw or two, Zac Keller. Anyone who's too perfect makes me nervous."

"You think I'm perfect?" he teased.

"I did, but now I know that you have an occasional selfish moment. It makes you seem more human."

"Well, don't talk to Cessy too much about me, she'll tell you so many flaws that I'll go from human to subhuman in record time."

"I doubt that, Zac. You are truly one of the nice guys."

The phrase *nice guy* set his teeth on edge. His ex had used the phrase when she'd broken up with him. *You're such a nice guy. I'm sure you'll find someone else, someone better.*

He couldn't help but remember the phrase, "nice guys finish last."

He pushed away the thought and tried to remain upbeat. Eli was available. He was available. They were going to spend the day together.

Nice guys sometimes finish first.

And if he had anything to say about it, this would be one of those times.

BEING WITH ZAC WAS EASY. Cecily and Ariel ran from store to store, while Eli and Zac trailed behind at a more sedate pace. They'd gone into one store that sold Waterford crystal and Zac had bought a beautiful frame. "My mom will love it," he said with a hint of embarrassment.

"Real men buy crystal frames," she'd assured him as they strolled together.

They went by a maternity shop, and part of Eli wanted to go in and look. She'd never been in one before. She'd never had the need, and never thought she would. She knew Zac would have obliged her, but she wasn't ready to confess.

She wasn't ready for anyone else to know.

She'd received a parental reprieve, and so for one more week, she'd hold on to her news and hopefully adjust even more to the idea of being a mother.

So she just walked past the maternity store. There would be plenty of time to shop at one later.

"So, fill me in about your siblings. Cecily is the youngest. You're the oldest."

"Then there's Seth. He's a cop in Erie— we don't see him much anymore." There was a sadness in his voice, telling her there was some kind of trouble with Seth. He didn't share, and she didn't ask.

"Next there's May," he continued. "She's in Pittsburgh trying to find herself. This week she's a waitress, I think. I've offered her a job at Keller's, but she wants to make it on her own. Then there's Dom. He's graduating from Pitt in the spring, then Layla, who's at Carlow University in Pittsburgh."

"Wow. How on earth did your mom manage all of you? Six kids. I can't imagine." Trying to wrap her brain around raising just one child was taxing at best.

"Mom's…" He paused. "She's all heart. We were the kids no one wanted to adopt. Older. Damaged. But Mom put us all together and made us a family."

"She sounds wonderful. And you are lucky."

Zac nodded. "I am. We all are, and we know it. And Mom is fantastic." He paused. "Are you going to the girls' basketball game tomorrow at the school?"

Eli planned on staying at home tomorrow to figure out how to turn her guest room into a nursery. It was just an idea. One she wasn't sure she was ready for. Having a baby's room in the house would make everything seem so much more real.

A girls' basketball game would be easier. "I might go."

"Great. So you can probably meet the whole Keller clan. It's sort of like taking medicine. Best to get it all over with at once."

"What a way to talk about your family," she mock-scolded. "I'm sure they're all lovely."

"If by lovely you mean loud, then yes. All of us. Maybe especially my dad, who likes listening to his music as loud as possible. Mom banned his CD player to the garage, but even then we'd hear the music inside the house. Mom would holler at him because it was so loud, and after he turned it down, he'd say, 'Loud? Why it was quieter than inside the house,' in a puzzled way. It was a standing joke. He was the only one who laughed, but it made him laugh every time. He was the king of one-liners. You'd say something like, 'My head hurts.' His favorite response? 'Does your face hurt?' When you said no, he'd add, ''Cause it's killing me.' He cracked himself up with that one as well."

Eli laughed. "He sounds like a riot."

"Now, he does. When you're fifteen and

on the phone with a girl, not so much. What about you? Your family?"

"Just me. An only child of two only children. Quiet. That's the best way to describe our house. Mom and Dad are great, though. I see them most every weekend when they're in town. This weekend's pass is a fluke." Unexpected, and just this once, welcomed.

"When they're in town?"

"They've become snow bunnies. Heading for Florida before the snow, and not coming back until it's long since melted. But even when they're down south, we're close."

"That's nice. One of Mom's cross-stitched sayings goes, 'It's not the size of the family, it's the size of its heart.' In our case, sounds like we both have big ones." He groaned. "Okay, I feel emasculated by saying that out loud."

Eli laughed. "No, you sounded sweet. And I find it hard to believe your mom had all those kids and still found time to cross-stitch?"

"Actually, there's something my mother made in every room at my place. One Christmas she made all us kids a cross-stitch that said, 'I didn't carry you for nine months, but once I met you, I knew you were mine. So, now I'll carry you in my heart for the rest of my life.'" His voice gave a little hitch.

"Oh, Zac, that's lovely."

He looked embarrassed. "I don't know why I told you that. That one's not in the public portion of the house."

They were standing in the middle of the mall. And without thinking about it, Eli took Zac's hand and gave it a light squeeze. "I'm glad you shared it."

"Hey, Zac."

Eli realized she was still holding Zac's hand and dropped it.

Cecily didn't seem to notice as she opened a bag and pulled out a top. "Look what I've got to wear after the game tomorrow."

Ariel stood behind her, bagless. Eli wished she could offer the girl money to buy a new top. But she was Ariel's teacher, and had already edged too close to the boundary that should exist between a student and teacher. Plus, she suspected Ariel was too proud to accept it.

Zac was scowling in the general direction of Cecily's shirt. "Where's the rest of it?"

"Funny. Ha. Ha. It's all there." She turned to Ariel. "My brother thinks he's Mr. Funny. He's so not."

"And you know Dad's worse than I am," Zac continued. "And you know what else? It's practically winter. Turtlenecks are in season."

"Funny. You're almost as funny as Dad now, Zac, and that means not at all." She turned back to Ariel. "Tell, him Ariel. Tell him this isn't bad."

"It's a very popular style, Mr. Keller."

"Seriously, Ariel, don't go calling him 'Mister.' I told you, it gives him a swollen head. Soon he'll expect all of us to be Mistering him all over the place. And Z-man, that's so not going to happen."

"Don't listen to Miss Incorrigible, Ariel." Zac tried to sound stern, but knew he didn't manage it well. "Before she can start a fight with me, why don't we all head over to Elephant and Castle for dinner."

"You're not saying much, Ms. Cartwright," Ariel said as they walked toward the car.

"I'm an only child, but even I know better than to get in middle of a brother-and-sister sniping war."

Cecily and Zac continued their banter as they traveled the short distance to the restaurant. And they kept it up even after they were seated in a booth, only letting up when the waitress came over. "Can I start you all out with something to drink?"

When it was Ariel's turn, she said, "Water."

"Oh, come on," Zac prompted. "We're celebrating your new job and Cecily's first game tomorrow. This one's on me. You can do better than water. How about a milk shake? It's got milk in it, so it's good for you."

"Strawberry, then," Ariel said.

Eli realized that Ariel had been worried about paying for the dinner. She could have kicked herself for not making sure Ariel knew the meal was on her. While the girls were busy talking, she nodded at Ariel and mouthed the word *thanks* in Zac's direction.

IT WAS SEVEN O'CLOCK when Zac drove to Keller's Market parking lot. They'd already dropped Ariel off at her aunt's and Cecily was in the backseat.

Zac got out and walked Eli to her car.

"Thanks for a wonderful day." Eli had so enjoyed not having to worry. She'd enjoyed listening to Zac and Cecily's playful arguing. She'd enjoyed the meal. It had been especially sweet to hear Ariel and Cecily yakking—just two teenagers talking about school. Her conversations with Ariel had centered around her pregnancy, her school-work and her job. The dinner reminded her that Ariel was still a girl. A girl in the process of growing up too fast. "Really, I had a great time."

"You didn't buy anything. I don't think I've ever been shopping with a woman who didn't buy anything."

Eli shook her head. "Maybe you've been shopping with the wrong women."

Zac laughed. "Maybe."

She unlocked the door and opened it. Zac still stood there. "Did I forget something?"

"You were considering coming to the game tomorrow. I could pick you up. You're on my way and car-pooling…we'd be saving the planet and all that." He hesitated. "That is, if you want to."

Wanting to drive with Zac had nothing to do with saving the planet, although Eli had tried to live green before green was the fashionable color. "That would be great."

"You'll have to give me your address."

She gave him her best teacher's look. "I thought you said I was on your way?"

"Eli, Whedon is at best a fifteen-minute

drive from border to border. Okay, that's an exaggeration. You could probably drive the circumference of the town in fifteen minutes, with time to spare. Everything is on my way."

Eli laughed even harder as she dug in her bag and pulled out a card. "Here you go."

"Always prepared. I like that in a woman." He pocketed the card. "I'll be there at one."

"I'll be ready."

Zac stood there as she started the car and pulled away. She glanced in her rearview mirror and saw him finally moving toward his own car.

She went directly home and had barely taken off her coat when the phone rang.

She kicked off her boots, exposing her favorite striped socks, and ran for the living room. "Hello?" she answered breathlessly.

"Are you okay? Nothing wrong with the baby?" Tucker asked, anxiousness in her voice.

"I'm fine. I just walked in the house and ran for the phone." She flipped on the lamp and sank down onto the couch.

"I wanted to see how it went with your parents."

"They canceled. So I went to Grove City and did some shopping at the outlet mall."

There was silence on the other end of the line. "What's up, Tuck?"

"I've been calling you all day. At home. On your cell."

She dug through her purse and found her cell phone at the bottom. "The battery's dead. Sorry."

"No problem." Tucker paused. "Want to do something tomorrow?"

"I could in the morning, or late afternoon. I have something at one."

"Something?"

Eli pulled her feet onto the couch and covered them with the throw. "A girl's basketball game at the high school."

"Oh, I like basketball." Tucker muffled the phone, as if she were putting her hand over the receiver. "Hey, Bart, want to go to the girls' basketball game tomorrow?"

Eli could hear Bart's voice, although she couldn't make out what he was saying.

Tucker came back on the line. "He says it's only a scrimmage, but sure. We'll meet you there, unless you want me to pick you up?"

Eli wasn't sure why she felt embarrassed, but she did as she replied, "I sort of have a ride already."

"Oh? With who?"

"Zac Keller. You remember, he's helping me out with the new CATA Project."

"Hot, single Zac Keller, whose family owns Keller's Market…the chain. That Zac Keller? You're *going with* Zac Keller?"

"Yes. It's only car-pooling. You know, to save the environment."

Tucker snorted. "Eli, you're a catch… pregnant or not."

"Shh! I don't want Bart to overhear you. I need to tell my parents before I tell anyone else."

"So what happened with telling them today?"

"They had unexpected plans and canceled. I'll tell them next week."

"You sure you don't want me to come with you when you do? Your parents always liked me, and maybe I'd serve as a reminder that unexpected pregnancies sometimes turn out to be a blessing in disguise. I could bring Bart's last report card. All A's…not that I'm bragging."

Eli laughed. "You're bragging. But mombrags look very good on you, Tuck. And thanks again for the offer, but I can handle this. More than anyone, I know how these things go."

"But it's not the same when it's you. When you're worried about your parents being disappointed in you."

"I'll handle it. I'll handle it all, Tuck."

"Just remember, you're not alone."

"I won't forget." Eli's hand rested on her stomach, and she thought it felt a little rounder.

She wasn't alone. Not ever. Friends. Family. And soon, a baby.

CHAPTER FOUR

"First things first. You need to tell those you love that you're pregnant. You're going to need their support."
—*Pregnancy, Childbirth and Parenting for Teens,* by Mary Jeanne Lorei

ZAC ARRIVED ON TIME to pick up Eli and held open her jacket. She looked startled. "Sorry. I know some women take offense, but my mom's lessons on how a gentleman should behave stuck."

"I don't ever take offense when none is meant." She stuck the hat on herself. "Okay, I'm good to go."

"Just like that? A jacket and hat—no primping? My sisters always take forever to get ready to go anywhere. Even just a basketball game."

"I might have when I was younger, but such is the way of age. You've figured some things out." Eli smiled as she opened the door, letting him go through first, then followed him and used the key to turn the dead bolt.

"Only some things? You always seem to have everything sorted and in order." He opened her car door.

Eli climbed in, saying, "If only you knew."

Zac walked around the car and got in the driver's side. "Ah, is that a cryptic reference to whatever was bothering you the other day? That offer to listen is still there."

She paused and looked him directly in the eye, as if seeing him for the first time. "I may take you up on that someday. But not today. Today is for basketball and Niagra pride."

The school parking lot was overflowing with cars. And as they made their way into the gym, the home side was awash with blue and white.

"There they are," Zac said, pointing to his family sitting in the bleachers. He did a quick head count. Everyone had made it, including Seth, although he sat apart from his parents. Cessy would be surprised and pleased.

"Hi, this is Eli. Eli, my mom and dad, Abe and Deborah Keller. And..." He listed each name, trying to see his family through Eli's eyes. Was she taking in the different colored skin, the lack of any similar features? Was she seeing the braces on Dom's legs?

"Eli, come sit by me," his mom invited, patting the spot next to her.

Eli went over and took the seat between his mom and May. There was no way Zac could squeeze in, too, so he sat behind them between Dom and Seth.

"Thanks for coming," he said to his brothers. "Cessy seemed to really need us all here."

"No problem." Dom nodded at Eli. "By the way, nice-looking lady."

Zac didn't say anything. He turned to the still silent Seth. "Thanks."

"I'm here for Cessy" was Seth's flat response.

Zac had tried in the past to mend the rift between his parents and Seth, but his brother would have none of it, and not wanting to start a fight today, he didn't say anything.

"You two serious?" Seth jerked his head in Eli's direction.

"She recently ended another relationship, but…"

Any further conversation was put on hold

as the home team entered the gym. Cessy was easy to spot. She towered over her teammates.

A woman and boy arrived and sat down by May, Eli and his mom. Zac realized he hadn't planned this very well. What he'd hoped would be a continuation of yesterday's good time wasn't working out that way.

"Hey, it's fine. You can go be with her at half time. I won't be insulted," Dom assured him.

"That obvious?"

Dom laughed. "Maybe not to everyone, but I'm not everyone. I'm your brother. And I am good at reading people. Even if I wasn't, you've always been pretty much an open book."

Zac laughed. It wasn't only Cessy who'd needed to connect with the family. He did, too.

He glanced over at Eli and she seemed totally relaxed with his mom. Good. He wanted her to fit in. He hoped she'd be spending a lot more time with them in the future.

THE GAME WENT FASTER than Eli thought it would. The home team won by three points.

Cecily Keller was an amazing player, especially for a freshman on the varsity team.

Eli had planned to ask Zac to drop her at home as soon as the game ended, but Mrs. Keller had proclaimed a family dinner was in order to celebrate the first scrimmage, and while Eli thought her I'm-not-family excuse should get her out of going, it didn't.

Tucker and Bart were dragged along, too.

"I could have told you arguing with my mother was useless," Zac explained as he escorted her into the rambling Keller home. They waited on the porch for Tucker and Bart to get out of their car and follow them.

"I don't think you two formally met. Angelina Tucker, this is Zac Keller. And this is Tucker's son, Bart."

Zac led them back to a huge kitchen and started introducing Tucker and Bart to his family. Even as he picked on his siblings the genuine affection was apparent.

Mrs. Keller pulled bowl after bowl out of the refrigerator, and took the lids off of two Crock-Pots. "Dig in, everyone."

It was chaos.

Pandemonium.

It was wonderful.

"Are you as freaked out by all these people

as I am?" Tucker asked as they sat together in a relatively quiet corner of the living room. Bart had disappeared with Cecily, leaving the adults on their own.

"You two hiding, too?" Zac's brother, Seth asked.

He was teasing. Until now, he'd been monosyllabic at best. Eli could sense there was some rift in the family, and Seth's avoidance of his parents confirmed that. It was like a dance. Every time his mother headed in his direction, he countered and moved in the opposite one.

"Do you need anything?" Seth continued, without waiting for either of them to respond to his first question.

"In your dreams," Tucker said with a scoff. "My son's got socks in his drawer that are older than you."

Seth looked flustered for a moment. "I didn't mean it that way—" he began, then saw Tucker was teasing and smiled. The expression looked a bit rusty, but he managed to tease back, "Hey, I'm a cop. I spend my life protecting and serving the community. That ages a man rapidly. Heck, I might be chronologically seven years younger than my big brother, but my soul is so much older than his paltry thirty-four years."

"Listen, Seth, you seem like a nice guy, but I'm not interested. And Eli's—"

For a second, a horrifying second, Eli thought Tucker was going to say she was pregnant. *And Eli is pregnant.* But when Tuck said, "And Eli isn't interested, either," Eli breathed a sigh of relief. She should have known better.

Eli laughed. "Sorry, Seth."

"Hey, you can't blame a guy for trying." He sat down on the couch next to Tucker. "But since I know you're not interested, you're safe. I'm hiding out with you two."

"I thought you were a big, brave cop. I didn't know that involved hiding."

"Sure it does. Don't you watch cop shows? They're always staking out someone…."

The two of them continued their banter, while Eli digested Seth's words. Zac was only thirty-four. Ten years younger than she was.

Not that it mattered. It wasn't as if there was anything more than a friendly business association between them. But still, she'd thought Zac was older. Around her age, at least.

"…Zac," Tucker said.

Eli had been too preoccupied to catch the

first part of Tucker's sentence, but Zac's name was enough to draw her back.

"That's how it goes. Zac always got all the girls because he was older."

Zac had somehow edged close to their conversation when she was lost in thought.

"Wrong, little brother," he corrected. "I got the girls because I was oh, so much prettier."

Eli studied him, and still didn't see a younger man. She just saw Zac. Someone who was a friend. A nice guy.

"I'm sure that's what they said, but they only said that to make you feel better about your rather large nose," Seth countered.

"You know what they say about men with big noses…?" Tuck started, then stopped. "Or maybe it was big hands."

"I think this conversation has gone about as far as I'm comfortable with," Eli said as primly as possible.

"Come on with me," Zac said. "These two can duke out the whole age issue without our help."

Eli couldn't see any way not to go with him and not seem rude, so she got up and followed him.

He led her to the back porch, which looked

out over a beautifully landscaped yard. "Does your mom do the gardening or your dad?"

"Both. After all these years, they still enjoy bumming around together. They consider working in the garden a date. Groceries, too. Us kids always called them geek dates, but it's actually sort of comforting knowing they still get along. Does that make sense?"

She nodded. "My parents are like that. A unit. I can't imagine one without the other. They're heading down to Florida in a few weeks. They love to call me with news of their adventures. Mom got Dad to try ballroom dancing lessons a few years ago, and now they like to hit the clubs. Picturing my mom and dad club-hopping is a bit bizarre."

"It's nice knowing people who can raise kids, and still maintain a sense of self. That's what I want someday."

Eli didn't nod, didn't say anything. Once upon a time, she'd have said the same thing. And not too long ago, she'd have said she'd found that with Arthur. But their relationship had been a sham.

And now with the baby coming?

She couldn't imagine she was going to be

able to balance her job and raising a child with finding a new boyfriend. So odds were, she was out of the running for that kind of relationship. The kind her parents and Zac's had.

The thought saddened her.

"I never called my parents' outings geek dates, but now that I know the term, I could. Antiques. Mom's crazy about antiques and Dad tends to indulge her. Those would probably qualify."

Zac grinned. "Do you like antiques?"

"Sure. I grew up with them. I don't know as much as my parents, but I have a fondness for old stoneware."

"I know a place in Mill Village, Abercrombie's. They've always got interesting things. Maybe we could drive out sometime."

Was he asking her for a date? She liked Zac. He made her laugh. But she wasn't ready to tell people she was pregnant, and once she did, she figured he wouldn't be interested in dates, if that's what this was.

"As just friends, right?"

"I'd like to think we're friends," he answered.

"Good. I can use all the friends I can get. But I'm not in the market for anything more than that. It's only been a few days since Arthur and I broke up." She felt a bit presumptuous saying it, but still she respected Zac and wanted to be honest. She didn't want to muddy the water of their friendship with unrealistic expectations.

He'd find out soon enough she was pregnant, and that would remove all her worries, but until she was ready to share the news, she wanted to be clear.

"Just friends." There was a hint of something in his voice as he said the words—something Eli couldn't quite identify.

Whatever it was, it made her heart do a weird little double beat. As if she could possibly be attracted to Zac Keller. But she wasn't. For a myriad of reasons she knew she wasn't attracted and never could be. They worked together on the CATA Project, he was younger, she was barely out of a long-term relationship…and she was pregnant. All good reasons to make sure their relationship stayed platonic.

She should say no to his invitation to Abercrombie's, but instead, she reiterated, "Friends," then found herself saying, "That sounds great."

"How about tomorrow, after you're done at school?"

"I have an appointment tomorrow after school." He gave her a look that said he thought she was trying to blow him off. She wasn't. So she quickly added, "But Tuesday would work."

"Tuesday it is."

TUESDAY AFTER SCHOOL, Eli waited for Zac in a chair by the window in her living room.

Her appointment yesterday had been a snap. They'd done a sonogram to get a measurement, and determine when the baby would be born. But Dr. Benton was pretty sure she'd have her baby toward the end of May. Eli would be able to work the school year, and spend the whole summer with the baby.

Her baby.

The idea still felt surreal, but she thought she was getting used to it.

Her hand drifted toward her stomach. The baby resembled a blob on the sonogram, and though the technician tried to point out things, no matter how much Eli tried, it was still a blob.

She heard Zac pull up out front.

He laughed as she hurried down the drive. "Wow, that was fast."

"I was watching for you. It's a beautiful day for a drive."

"So, how did your appointment go yesterday?" he asked as they started towards I-79.

She tried to remember what she'd told him, but couldn't, so she simply said, "Fine."

"And how are you doing…I mean with the breakup and all."

The breakup.

Arthur.

She hadn't heard from him and—she hated to admit it, even to herself—barely thought of him since she'd told him about the baby and he'd bailed.

What kind of person did that make her?

She dated Arthur Stone for five long years, and she hadn't felt the loss of the relationship.

Hadn't missed him.

"Hey, you got really quiet. Are you sure everything's okay?"

"Just thinking. It's a teacher's curse. You can leave the school building, but you never quit working."

"So, how goes CATA?"

"I have two other businesses interested and…" She babbled about her job, because in truth, it was easier to think about that than think about everything else.

Maybe that's why she'd agreed to go out with Zac today. He didn't know about the baby, so there were no sympathetic looks like she got from Tucker, there was no shock like there had been with Arthur, and there was no nervousness that she hadn't told him yet like there would have been with her parents.

He was just Zac. A nice guy who was a friend.

And she was just Eli. Someone who liked antiques. Someone who enjoyed a drive on a fall afternoon.

The rest of it…she'd worry about that later.

Specifically this weekend, when she saw her parents.

FOR THE FIRST TIME IN her adult life, the weekend came too soon, in Eli's estimation.

"Mom, Dad…" Eli started as she sat across from them in her very neat living room.

She'd practiced her speech over and over again. She knew what she had to say, but she wasn't sure she was ready for what would follow.

She stared at them. Gail and John Cartwright. Childhood sweethearts who still held hands, as they did now, sitting on her sofa. Both wore expressions of trepidation. She worried that she'd scared them with her opening: I've got big news.

"Listen, you know I love you. You've tried to raise me right and I appreciate that. I've tried to live up to the ideals you set for me. What I'm going to tell you might upset you. And though it's certainly not what I planned…"

She paused.

She'd been here before so many times. Only *she'd* been the moral support for a girl who was telling her parents she was going to be a teen mother. She tried to remember her advice.

Tell your parents you love them, and that though this wasn't what any of you had planned, this baby is a gift and you're going to do everything you can to be worthy of the life that's been entrusted to you.

"And though I know this isn't what I had planned, I have to tell you that I'm…"

The word *pregnant* hung for a second on the tip of her tongue. Once she said it, once it was out in the open, everything would change.

"I'm pregnant."

Her mother clapped her hands to her mouth and her father sat stone-faced and unreadable.

"Mom. Dad. Say something. Say anything." She waited for them to tell her how disappointed they were. That this wasn't how they'd raised her.

"Oh, Eli…"

Wait for it. Wait for it, she commanded herself, steeling herself for her mother's words.

"I'm going to be a grandmother." Her mother hugged herself with apparent glee. "Oh, my. I'd given up hope. Will I be Grandma? Grammy? Granny—no. I hate that one. Mammy? Nana? Bubbi?" The words rushed over one another, tripping to get out.

Her mother sprang from the couch as if she were too excited to stay still any longer. She hugged Eli tight.

"Mom—" *You're happy* was what she was going to say, but her mother interrupted.

"Oh, Eli, I'm going to be a grandmother."

She took a deep breath that Eli could feel, as she was still caught in her mother's death-grip of a hug.

"Gail, I don't think Eli can breathe," her

father said. "And that can't be good for the baby."

Her mother let go immediately.

"Come and take a seat, honey, before you keel over." Her father made room for her on the sofa next to him. "Congratulations, Eli." He smiled, but his brows puckered in such a way that she could tell he was worried.

There was no puckering, no worry in her mom's expression, as she asked, "Now, when's your due date? Do you know?"

"May."

"Why isn't Arthur here with you, telling us?" her father asked.

There it was again, the pucker.

Well, they'd taken the news about the baby better than she'd imagined, so maybe they'd take the news about Arthur better as well.

"You see, Arthur's not going to be a part of this. We broke up and—" *I'm doing this on my own* was going to be the rest of the sentence, but her doorbell rang and interrupted her. "Hang on a minute."

Eli hurried to the door. Zac was there, with pizza boxes and a DVD. "Hey, I brought food, hoping it would keep you from being annoyed that I've just dropped by uninvited and unannounced."

She heard her parents' footsteps and knew they'd followed her. She turned and they were standing in the doorway studying Zac.

"Mom, Dad, this is my friend, Zac Keller. Zac, my parents, John and Gail Cartwright."

Zac handed Eli the pizzas and walked up to her parents. "Mr. and Mrs. Cartwright, it's so nice to meet you. Eli's said such lovely things about you. My mother totally fell for Eli when she was over, and said her parents must be wonderful to have raised such a great daughter."

Her mother looked hurt. "You told his family first?"

"Told my family what?" Zac looked confused.

Eli realized that her mother had misunderstood. "Mom, it's not what you think. I—"

Her father cleared his throat and interrupted. "Elinore, you know we've always supported you and your decisions. And though we haven't seen Arthur in a few months, it didn't sound as if you'd been separated very long. After all, today is the first you've mentioned it. So how long could you have known this man? This is a monumental undertaking for two practical strangers."

She was in trouble when she was Elinore.

"Dad, I—"

This time Zac interrupted. "Mr. Cartwright, Eli and I have worked together for quite a while on her new CATA Project. Now that it's time to implement it, well, so far so good. We've become quite close. She's an amazing woman."

"The CATA Project is a huge undertaking," her mother said. "But John's talking about the baby."

"What baby?" Zac asked, clearly baffled.

"Yours and Eli's," her father responded, looking stern. "And I need to ask you, sir, what are your intentions with my daughter?"

"Baby?" Zac asked Eli.

She nodded. "We'll talk later. But Mom, Dad, this is ridiculous. Zac's not—"

"Afraid to answer your question, Mr. Cartwright," Zac finished. "My intentions, in regard to your daughter, are to do whatever she wants to make this easier on her. I've liked her longer than she knows."

"Liked her?"

"More than like, if I were honest, but I'm taking it slow, so as not to frighten Eli off."

"You two obviously didn't take it slow enough," her father groused.

"Enough," Eli said loudly. "Everyone keeps interrupting me. I am not some child who needs to be defended, or explained."

"Yes, exactly." Her mother came over and put an arm gently around Eli. "Enough, you men. My daughter's pregnant and I'm thrilled. I have so much to do. So much to think about. I have to learn to knit, and we'll have to go shopping for the baby. Oh, Eli, I've wanted to be a grandmother for so long."

Eli was on the verge of telling all of them that the baby was Arthur's, but her mother's last statement stopped her. "Really?"

"Oh, yes."

"But you never said anything."

"I wouldn't want you to feel as if I were disappointed that I wasn't. I didn't want to pressure you. But no matter how this baby came about, know it's going to be loved and spoiled beyond all sense and reason." She glanced at Zac. "And no matter how long you've known the father, we'll accept him, too."

Her mother walked over to Zac and hugged him. "Welcome to the family, son."

"Stop. Please. Zac. Is. Not. The. Baby's.

Daddy." She enunciated each word as clearly and succinctly as she could.

"Eli and I are friends who are working our way up to dating," Zac added helpfully. "But I'm thrilled about the baby. I have five siblings, and am pretty handy with babies, if I do say so myself."

"You dumped Arthur, got pregnant by someone else and now are dating this man?" Her father's voice held a sad disbelief.

"No. I didn't dump Arthur. He dumped me and the baby—his baby. And I'm not dating Zac."

"Not yet, but hey, a guy can hope." Zac grinned.

What on earth was with him? Eli gave him a sharp jab with her elbow.

Her parents both looked as confused as she felt. "Gail, I think we'd better go and let these two work out what's going on with them."

"You're right, John." She hurried to Eli and swept her into her arms. "No matter who the baby's father is or isn't, or how long you've known him, don't you worry. Your father and I are here for you every step of the way. And…" She squeezed Eli tighter. "Eli, a baby. I'm beside myself with happiness."

Suddenly her mother's face clouded over.

"John, we were leaving in a week for Florida. I don't know if I can go now. Eli might need me. I—"

"Mom, Florida's a couple hours' flight. I don't want this to undo any of your plans. You'll be home long before the baby comes."

"But I—"

"Gail, we'll talk about Florida and what Eli does and doesn't need from us later."

For a moment, Eli wasn't sure her mother was going to agree, but then she slowly nodded. "Okay. Tomorrow, Eli. I'll talk to you tomorrow after you and Zac here sort things out." She turned to Zac. "It was very nice to meet you, young man. We never really liked Arthur, you know."

And with that surprising last sentence, her mother took her father by the hand and said, "Come on, John. Let's take a drive into Erie and do some shopping on Peach Street. We can stop at Babies 'R' Us and then…"

The rest of her mother's plans were muted as they closed the door.

Zac took back his pizzas from Eli and started walking toward her kitchen. There was nothing left for her to do but follow and ask, "What on earth was that all about?"

He set the boxes on the counter. "What?"

"Don't *what* me. You didn't come right out and deny the baby was yours. And then you claimed we were dating. We are not dating."

He opened up one of the lids. "Do you want to get us plates?"

On autopilot, she opened the cupboard, grabbed two plates, then took a handful of napkins back to the island's counter.

"So what gives?"

"A," he began, as he put a piece of pizza on a plate and slid it in front of Eli, "I didn't know you were pregnant, and didn't know the circumstances with your parents. So I just tried to go along with it."

"I didn't ask you—"

"And B," he said, taking the other plate and another piece of pizza and sliding it in front of himself, "we haven't been dating only because I wanted to give you time to get over your breakup with Arthur. I have no interest in becoming your rebound guy, but I'm every bit interested in dating you for a long time to come. I was trying to be considerate and ease you into the notion."

"Well, you can obviously see that's out of the question now. I thought it was just friendship, Zac. If I'd known you were hoping it was anything else, I would have said something and put a stop to it. Truth is, I was selfish. I had fun hanging out with you. It was easy to forget…well, everything. All the changes I'll be going through—my life will be going through. The time we were together I wasn't worrying about the future, about how I'm going to handle becoming a mother. I'm sorry. You deserve so much more than that."

"And you deserve all the friends and support you can get. If you don't mind me asking, if you're having his baby, why did you break up with Arthur?" Zac took a bite of his pizza.

"I had a choice. Arthur or the baby. I chose the baby."

He dropped the pizza back onto the plate, swallowed and asked, "He didn't want it?"

"He's got his life mapped out and this wasn't on the map."

"So, did you…you didn't plan on a baby?"

"Once upon a time, I thought I'd have a houseful of kids. I never found the right guy, and it was never the right time. So somewhere along the line, I decided it wasn't going to happen and I've set up a quiet life for myself."

"That's going to change real fast." Zac

chuckled. "I've got younger siblings and I can assure you, babies aren't quiet."

"No, they're not—I do know that much. But it's a drop in the bucket compared to what I don't know. You'd think the fact I've done this, dealt with situations like this, for years, that I'd have it all together. I don't, I've got a lot to figure out. And I will. I've watched too many girls cry because they're pregnant. I won't do that. This baby might be unexpected, but it's being greeted with…" She searched for the right word. *Joy* wasn't quite it. "It's being welcomed."

Zac nodded, as if he'd never doubted it for a moment. "Eli, I want to keep seeing you."

"As friends," she clarified.

"I want to see you in whatever capacity you'll allow me to," he said.

"I don't want to lead you on, Zac. I've got a lot on my plate. We can be friends, but there's too much stacked against us being anything more. If that can be enough, then yes."

"Fine. If that's what you want."

"That's what I want," she assured him.

"Then friends it is."

A COUPLE OF HOURS LATER, Zac turned off the television. It was ironic that he'd thought to woo Eli by bringing a chick-flick movie disguised as an action-adventure, called *Adventures in Friendship*. Two best friends cavorting through Europe, running from the big bad mafia and discovering they have deep romantic feelings for each other.

He wondered if there were any mafia guys interested in chasing after a grocery store manager and a teacher. Maybe that would convince Eli they could still be a couple.

But she was pregnant.

A baby.

The news was a shock, and he wasn't quite sure what to do about it.

"Zac, I don't want to be rude, but I really have some things to get done around the house, and I expect my mother and father to stop by once she's done buying out every baby store on Peach Street."

He took the hint. "Yeah, I'd better go."

She stood at her door, watching him walk to his car. He wanted nothing more than to go back, hold her and tell her everything would be all right.

But he'd wait.

Zac had gotten very good at waiting.

Rather than drive home though, he went to his parents'. It was never quiet there, and he wanted something to distract him.

He found his mom in the kitchen, which was no surprise. The fact that he didn't see his dad or sister, was.

"Where's the gang?"

"Cessy had basketball practice, and your father's picking her up."

His mother was stirring a pot of something as he sat down at the island counter. "You'll stay for dinner?"

He meant to say "Yeah, of course." Instead, he blurted out, "Eli's pregnant."

His mother stopped stirring and took the stool opposite him. "And what are you two going to do."

"No, it's not mine. It's her ex's. He found out and dumped her."

"I'm sorry. That has to be hard on her."

"Mom, does it make me lower than low to be glad he's gone? Even knowing about the baby? I know I should hope they get back together, but I can't."

She studied him for a long moment. "You care about her." It was a statement, not a question.

"I have for a long time. While he was in

the picture, I let it go. But now? I know that her being pregnant with another man's baby should change things, but it doesn't. I still want her. I still want to date her, to get closer to her. But a baby. Someone else's baby? She says she can't do that to me."

"Zac, the heart doesn't care about such things. If you like Eli, her being pregnant doesn't change that. Maybe it adds complication, but life's complicated, and so are relationships.

"Your father and I wanted many children, and when that didn't happen we decided that maybe our children weren't going to grow in my womb. Maybe they were out there waiting for us. So we contacted social services. They told us you weren't clear to be adopted, but we could foster you, that they expected your biological parents' rights to be terminated. And I said yes.

"There you were, Zachary Manhiem, a tiny little boy with dark brown hair that sorely needed a trim. Your clothes were too small, and your expression was too guarded. But I knew—I knew as soon as I saw you that you were ours."

"I remember that day." He couldn't remember the last time he'd eaten, and he'd never been to school. Someone in the neighborhood had called and reported his mother to social services. He'd never known who, but he owed whoever it was a debt of gratitude.

When he'd gone to the group home, the only thing he'd brought from his past was a piggy bank.

"You were so small, yet so old. You kept your distance. You were polite. Quiet. You always did what you were asked. You had a way of looking at me and your dad, as if you were assessing us. You were careful.

"A few months after you arrived, you started school. That first day, when I came to get you, you said—"

"I didn't think you'd come."

"And I told you that I'd always come get you, that you were my son and I loved you." There were tears in her eyes, even after all these years.

"That Christmas I told you the stories of Christmas and Chanukah, trying to blend your traditions with ours. You asked what you were. And I told you—"

"That I could be whatever I wanted to be. And I said, I want to be a Keller. I want to be your son."

"You chose to be Zachary Keller. A man of honor, of heart. A man I'm so proud to call my son. About Eli and her baby, give it time. You've always made good decisions and pursued them with no doubts, no hesitation. Some people take longer. Eli's experiencing so much change right now. Patience. If it's love, you'll both figure it out."

"We haven't known each other long enough to use the L word."

"So, you'll see each other more and figure out if you should use the L word. Because if you love Eli, I'm sure you'll fall in love with this baby. Our family knows, so much more than most, that a family isn't tied by genetics, it's tied by love. If you're meant to be a family, you'll find a way."

"So, I should date her regardless?"

"Be her friend. It sounds like she could use them right now. Then see what happens." His mother echoed Eli's words.

"So, I'll be her friend."

His mom was right, Eli could use all the friends she could get. For now, that's what he'd be. And later? Well, they'd see.

CHAPTER FIVE

"The second trimester is a time of change. Most mothers feel wonderful during these months. The morning sickness and excessive tiredness of the first trimester has diminished. Women feel good. They're starting to become used to the idea of the baby."
—*Pregnancy, Childbirth and Parenting for Teens,* by Mary Jeanne Lorei

ELI STRAIGHTENED THE CORNUCOPIA in the center of her table. Last month she'd sworn that Halloween was her favorite holiday, but looking at her house all decorated for Thanksgiving, she had to confess, Thanksgiving might be, after all.

Her hand drifted to her stomach.

Her baby.

Next year at this time, she'd be putting the

cornucopia on the table while holding the baby on her hip.

She could see it in her mind's eye. How often she'd realized that this time next year, she'd have a baby. It was easy to imagine.

She was getting used to the idea of the baby.

And she was getting used to having Zac around.

He was coming to pick her up soon.

She'd talked to her mom this morning. Her parents had settled back into their Florida home, but unlike most years, her mother kept hemming and hawing about coming back to Pennsylvania because she was worried about Eli. Eli spent most conversations assuring her mother she was fine, and today's call was no exception. Her mom worried about her being alone on Thanksgiving, but Eli assured her that she would be with the Kellers, and with so many Kellers, there was no way she'd be alone.

The doorbell rang as if on cue, and she said goodbye to her mother and hurried to the door. She glanced at her watch. He was early, but she was happy. That pretty much summed up her relationship with Zac. When he was around, she was simply happy.

She threw the door open...and froze. "Arthur?"

Her bubble of happiness popped.

"Is this a bad time?" He looked as if he were hoping she'd say yes it was a bad time. Worse than that, he looked downright queasy.

Good mothers think about what's best for their baby, not what's best for themselves. Knowing the father was what was best for her baby, she'd need to make an effort when it came to Arthur. "It's fine. Come in."

She opened the door wider for him.

It had been a little more than a month since she'd seen him. She waited for the pang of longing, for some feeling of regret that things turned out the way they had. When those emotions didn't surface, she waited to feel fury—he'd treated her badly, and treated their unborn baby worse.

Still, she felt nothing, except maybe a sense of wonder about what she'd ever seen in him.

Should she offer him a drink? She didn't know what the protocol was when dealing with an ex-lover who'd abandoned you and your unborn child.

"Did you want something, Arthur? Did you bring the papers from the lawyer, perhaps?" she finally asked. She didn't see any papers, but maybe they were tucked inside his coat.

"No. I haven't been to the lawyer yet." He sounded almost angry at her.

Maybe that's why her hackles were up as she countered, "Then why are you here?"

"I missed you. I worried about you. I came to see how you were doing." There was still no tenderness in his admission.

He'd only mentioned her, which annoyed her even more. Arthur could ignore the baby, but she couldn't—wouldn't. "I'm doing fine. And the baby's doing fine, not that you asked."

"This was a mistake. I just wanted to see how you were doing," he repeated. He turned as if to leave.

"Arthur."

He stopped, hand on the doorknob, and faced her.

"Arthur, what do you really want?"

He ran his fingers through his always well-styled hair, leaving it mussed. "I don't know, Eli. I know what I don't want more than what I do want."

"What don't you want?"

Slowly, quietly, he said, "I don't want a baby. I don't want our lives to change. I don't want to lose you, but if you're keeping the baby, I don't know how to keep you."

"I'm sorry, Arthur." And as she said the words, her annoyance with him faded. She *was* sorry. Sorry that she'd wasted five years of her life on this man. Sorry that he couldn't see what a blessing this baby could be.

"Arthur, keeping me is out of the question, no matter what you do from here on out. We're over. There will be no reconciliation. However, if you decide you want to be part of the baby's life…" She let the offer hang there.

He ignored her mention of the baby, and honed in on her comment about their relationship. "You can't just write off a five-year relationship."

"I didn't, you did."

"Eli—" He stopped, as if he didn't know what to say.

So Eli said the words that had to be said. "Arthur, you and I? It's done. There's no going back." And to herself, she admitted that she didn't want to go back. She didn't miss Arthur the way she should if she truly loved him. "But whether you're a dad who takes an active role in the baby's day-to-day life, or a father who spends a few days here and there with the baby, I'll work with you. Children should know their fathers."

The books said so. Studies said so. And Eli had seen enough teen relationships to know that most of the time it was better if a child's father was present.

"I want *you,*" he blustered with a petulant whine in his voice.

She gritted her teeth at the sound, but didn't address his childishness. "Arthur, I don't mean to be cruel, but I don't want you carrying around false hope—I don't want you."

His face blanched at the baldness of her words. "I—"

"Go figure out what you want as far as the baby is concerned. That's the only decision you have in front of you. Either you want to play a role in his or her life, or you're going to the lawyer and terminate your parental rights."

"Eli…" He just stood there, undecided.

"It's all right, Arthur," she said with gentleness. "You take some time and figure it out. Right now, you have to go. I'm waiting for someone."

"A date?"

"A friend," she corrected.

"A male friend?"

She nodded, unsure where this jealousy was coming from. Arthur had been many things during their relationship, but jealous was never one of them. "A colleague," she clarified. "And a friend."

"A friend who's coming over on Thanksgiving? Friendly colleagues don't tend to share holidays with each other."

"Arthur, I don't have to explain myself to you. You lost the right—if you ever had it— to approve my itinerary when we broke up. Now, if you'll excuse me." She opened the door as a not-so-subtle hint. Cold November air rushed into the hallway.

It would snow soon.

She was sending her boyfriend of five years packing, and rather than crying, she was thinking about the weather.

"Eli—"

"Goodbye, Arthur. Figure out what you want to do and get back to me."

"Can I call and check on you?"

"No, but you can call and check on the baby."

As she held the door open, she saw Zac pull up on the street in front of her house since Arthur's car was parked in the driveway.

Arthur saw her looking past him and turned to look as well. "That him?"

"Go home, Arthur."

Arthur didn't move. He waited until Zac got up to the door. "Arthur Stone," he said, extending his hand.

Zac didn't take it. "Zac Keller."

"Him?" Arthur asked again.

"Go home, Arthur" was her flat response.

Arthur finally took his cue and started toward his car.

"Sorry," Eli said to Zac.

"You don't have anything to apologize for."

"Maybe not, but I feel as if I should. Come on in, while I get bundled up."

"How was your day?" he asked.

"Nice. Well, until about ten minutes ago."

He jerked his head in the general direction of her driveway. "Did he give you trouble?"

"No. Not trouble, really. He's just confused. He doesn't want the baby, but he still wants me."

"And you, what do you want?"

ZAC HELD HIS BREATH AFTER he'd asked the question and forced himself to exhale. He knew that he wasn't officially dating Eli, but this last month they'd spent a lot of time together. Basketball games. Sunday dinners with his family. He'd even had dinner at her parents' before they left for Florida.

No, they weren't dating, but they were creeping ever closer. He'd felt a sense of certainty that it was only a matter of time until they were officially a couple.

And now Arthur was back.

What did this mean?

"I told Arthur that *us* wasn't an option. In fact, *us* wasn't ever a viable long-term option."

"You were together for five years," he declared, not so much because he wanted to remind her, but because he wanted to understand.

"Yes. Being with Arthur was easy. It didn't require any work. Any commitment. We had regular nights we were together, and we both did our own things as well. And I'll confess, on the nights I didn't see him, I didn't pine over him. There should be some pining in a good relationship, don't you think?"

Zac wasn't sure *pining* was the word he'd use for the days he didn't see Eli, but he did miss her when they weren't together. He wasn't sure that she'd recently analyzed their growing friendship, and he didn't push her to.

Rather than answer her pining question, he said, "So, are you ready to head to Mom and Dad's? The whole crew is going to be there."

The trip to his parents' was a quick one. They stopped to pick up Ariel from her aunt's, since the teen wasn't invited to her family's celebration. Zac couldn't understand how any parent could cut a child off so completely. He could imagine being disappointed, or even angry, but he'd still want to be there for his child. When Marge at the store mentioned that Ariel's aunt, an airline attendant, would be out of town, and her parents hadn't invited her home, Zac had issued the invitation.

Despite their age differences, Ariel had grown close to Cessy, and he was pretty sure it was Cessy who'd convinced Ariel to accept their invitation to Thanksgiving dinner.

"Thanks, Mr. Keller. Hi, Miss Cartwright," she'd said as she climbed into the backseat.

Ariel and Eli chatted the rest of the trip.

His parents' house was awash in light as they pulled up in front. A huge autumn leaf wreath hung heavily on the front door and thwapped against it as Zac threw the door open. He didn't need to call out or check what room they were in, they merely followed the dull roar.

"Z-man," Cessy cried as she ran across the kitchen floor. "You brought her. Hey, Ariel, Ms. Cartwright."

"Hi, Cecily." Eli smiled as Cessy engulfed Ariel in a huge hug.

"Thanks for not calling me Cessy, Ms, Cartwright. Some people—" her voice rose in volume as she said the words, leaving no doubt that her family was some people "—can't seem to remember I'm not four."

"Sorry, squirt, you'll always be four to us," Zac said and tweaked a hair that had strayed from her ponytail.

"Squirt?" Cessy stood up straight.

The whole family started discussing Cessy's squirtness and Zac saw his mother come up to Eli and talk to her quietly.

Cessy dragged poor Ariel down the hall, presumably to her room.

Zac found a quiet corner and just observed. He loved that his family had embraced Eli as one of their own. She tried to help with the dinner preparations, but they all kept telling her to sit down and put her feet up.

Zac followed her when she finally gave up and pulled up a chair in the family room. "They like you."

She snorted. "Maybe, but they won't believe I'm not an invalid."

"None of us have ever really been around a pregnant woman. I mean, we've done babies. I can remember when Cessy came home. She was so tiny and, Eli, she had so much hair, we all swore it weighed more than she did. They're just worried about you."

"When you put it that way, I suppose I'll have to content myself with being waited on."

As if on cue, Seth came in and handed Eli a glass of something red. "Cranberry juice. Mom said to tell you it's all juice and organic and that you should drink it."

"If you don't like cranberry juice, we'll cover for you," Zac said.

Eli laughed. "No, the baby and I like it just fine."

At the mention of the baby, Seth visibly winced and hurried back to the general pandemonium.

"Did I say something?"

"No, it wasn't you." Zac toyed with how

much to say, and opted to leave it at that. Today wasn't a day for sad stories, it was a day for family and giving thanks.

Zac didn't get to keep Eli to himself for long. His sisters arrived en masse and swooped Eli away. "Mom might not let you lift a finger, but come into the kitchen and visit with us."

Zac got up and found his brothers and Dad in the garage. "It's safe," Dom called. "Come on in, quick before they follow you."

They were all gathered around his father's ancient black-and-white television, that had a screen comparable to the size of an iPod's screen.

"Seriously, guys, why watch the game on this, instead of on the flat-screen in the family room?" Zac asked.

"Now, Zac, you know your mother never ventures out here if she can help it. We're hiding until the meal's served."

"She'd find us too quickly in the family room," Dom added, then laughed. "She's scary when it comes to the holidays. Do you remember that holiday she wanted to take a picture of all of us in front of the Christmas tree, with a menorah in the shot?"

"I have that picture as my screen saver," his

dad admitted. "And it wasn't so bad. I had the fire extinguisher in hand before the fire spread from that one branch."

They all laughed. Well, everyone except Seth, who might have had a small smile. It was hard to tell.

They crowded around the small TV, watching the college football game and sharing family stories until his mom came to the door and called. "I knew you were all hiding. But that's okay. The girls and I decided since we got dinner on the table, you all get to do dishes."

They laughed and followed their dad into the house. That's what Zac associated the most with being home—laughter. And as they all gathered around the table and gorged themselves on turkey and all the trimmings, there was a lot of laughter. A lot of noise. Eli and Ariel seemed to fit right in, both joining in the conversations. His parents had an awful habit of sharing embarrassing childhood stories, not just of him, but of all his siblings.

"You just wait, you two," his mom said to both Ariel and Eli. "One minute you're holding the most precious baby in the world in your arms, and the next, they're twelve and you're getting a call from the neighbors because they've climbed out their bedroom window… again."

"Ah, come on, Mom," Cessy cried right on cue. "Are you ever going to let me live it down?"

"Darling, I told you somewhere around the second time I caught you at it that I wouldn't."

Cessy turned to Ariel and Eli, who were sitting next to each other on the opposite side of the table. "I thought my biological mother might have been an alien and that's why she left me. I was hoping my alien superpower was flying."

Their whole family knew why Cessy's alien fantasies didn't include her father. Zac felt the familiar sense of pain as he remembered.

"Turns out her only alien superpower was annoying her older brothers," Dom, ever the peacemaker, teased in hopes of making everyone let go of the sad memory and laugh.

It worked.

Zac glanced at Eli. She gave him a look that said she'd caught the awkward moment, and that she was sorry, but she didn't ask any questions. And Zac knew she wouldn't. She would let him tell her when and if he was ready.

He smiled and gave a small nod, letting her know it was okay. Then he glanced at her plate, specifically at the place where his mother's dressing had been, but was now conspicuously empty. He glanced at her with a question in his eyes. She nodded.

He reached for the bowl that was in front of him. "Hey, Mom, can you pass this to Eli?"

"Your dressing's delicious, Mrs. Keller."

"It's the chestnuts. They give it just the right crunch."

"Hey, Zac, how did you know Eli wanted the dressing?" Cessy asked. "Maybe I wasn't the only alien Mom and Dad adopted. Me and my flying abilities, and you and your ESP."

"Nah, they've got that same thing Mom and Dad have. That conversations-with-their-eyes thing," Layla assured her. "I've always thought I don't want a guy who can't talk to me without saying a word."

"And I assure you, Lay, that most men I know would soooooo—" Dom drew the word out to annoy her especially "—appreciate having their only speech with you confined to ones without words."

Layla tossed a dinner roll at him.

He picked it up, poised to toss it back, when their mom said, "Children, we have guests."

And there it was, that look Layla had been talking about. His mom looked at his dad, and though both of them maintained a stern expression, they were laughing with each other.

They were talking without saying a word.

In that one quick glance between his parents, he'd seen not only their amusement, but also the love they had for each and for the family they'd built.

In Eli, he could see she'd seen his parents, and that she was as touched as he was.

Zac had dated women before, but he'd never met anyone he felt he could build a relationship with like his parents'.

Until now.

And as they resumed their regular holiday chatter, Zac acknowledged that he was most thankful for that sense of potential he had with Eli.

LATER THAT NIGHT, AFTER they'd dropped Ariel off at her aunt's, Zac pulled up in front of Eli's house.

She was exhausted, but she lingered in the car, not wanting the day to officially end. "I'm supposed to tell you thank you from my mom for rescuing me from a solo Thanksgiving."

"Did you tell her that Tucker invited you, too?"

"Oh, she knew. But if you've ever eaten Tucker's cooking, you'd know you did indeed rescue me." Tucker was great with a paintbrush in hand, but give her a pair of oven mitts and watch out.

"So, I have a long weekend for the holiday," Zac said. "I've got to check in at the store tomorrow morning, but the rest of the day is mine. What if I come pick you up and take you to lunch?"

"Zac, you must have better things to do."

"You say that every time I ask to spend time with you. Since my sister is convinced we can talk without talking, just like my parents, want to guess what I'm saying without saying?"

Eli tried to look serious, but all she could do was laugh. That seemed to be a common theme with Zac. They talked, they enjoyed each other's company and they both laughed a lot.

"Okay, tomorrow for lunch." She opened the door. "I'd better get in."

Before she got out, Zac leaned over and kissed her cheek. It was light, platonic even, and yet, she felt a bit breathless in a way that had nothing to do with the blast of cold air that flooded the car.

"Uh, well, thanks for a lovely day, Zac. I'd really best get in."

And in his eyes, without him saying a word, she could see that he knew his light buss on the cheek had flustered her, and that he was pleased.

She brushed a fingertip over the spot as she opened the door.

What was she going to do about Zac Keller?

CHAPTER SIX

"Holidays and family gatherings can be a very busy time, and an especially trying time for a pregnant mother. You can do as much as you're comfortable doing, but remember to pace yourself."
—*Pregnancy, Childbirth and Parenting for Teens,* by Mary Jeanne Lorei

THE TIME BETWEEN THANKSGIVING and the Christmas break always flew by, in Eli's opinion.

Fall leaves and turkeys were replaced by Christmas lights and evergreens. Eli left for school in the dark, and it was dusk by the time she got home most evenings.

She sat at her desk before first period looking out at the grayish sky and admitted to herself that she was nervous.

Today was the day she was going to break the news to her students that she was expecting a baby. She'd made an appointment with Barry Werner, the principal, and told him this morning. Afterward, she'd told a few teachers, and knew that with the way the school grapevine worked, the entire faculty would know by now.

That left her students. And really, her stomach was in knots at the thought of telling them. It was ridiculous and she realized it. She was an adult. She didn't have to make excuses to anyone. And yet…

Knot upon knot.

The bell for first period rang, and slowly, the girls filed in the room, one by one or in small clusters.

She had fifteen girls this year in her teen parenting class. Eli had other more traditional family and consumer science classes, but this one was nearest and dearest to her heart. Some of the girls, like Ariel, were pregnant, some already had babies. There were freshmen through seniors.

The room's volume had risen with their murmured conversations.

"Okay, everyone, find your seats."

Rather than abating, the noise grew even louder. Eli waited and everyone eventually sat down and looked at her expectantly.

"Thanks. Now, before we get started on today's lesson, I have some news I'd like to share with you all."

The girls were staring at her, and Eli realized her hand was placed protectively over her stomach. "For so many years I've worked in the teen pregnancy program, teaching parenting and life skills. It was rather ironic, since I'm single and childless. Well, I'm still single, but I'm very happy to announce—" and as she said the words, it occurred to her that despite her nervousness, she really *was* happy to announce "—I'll be remedying the childless part in May."

The noise level rose again as the girls babbled their congratulations. Eli glanced at Ariel, who was resolutely staring at her desk and not meeting Eli's eyes.

A couple of hands flew up, and Eli didn't have time to ponder Ariel's reaction. She called on Felicity.

"Ms. Cartwright, are you going to get married to the baby's father?"

Eli had anticipated this question and had given her response plenty of thought beforehand. "In an ideal world, a child's parents are married. But you all know from personal experience that this is not an ideal world. So, to answer your question, no. I'm not planning to marry the baby's father. We'd been in a long-term relationship, but marriage is not in our future."

"He dumped you?" Kelissa asked.

"I wouldn't say that," Eli hedged.

Kelissa looked furious on Eli's behalf. "He didn't want nothing to do with a baby and he dumped you. Just like me. My baby's no-good daddy doesn't want nothing to do with me or the baby. That's fine. You've taught me to be independent, and I'm going to look after this baby on my own. You'll do fine, too, Ms. Cartwright, you know more than all of us put together. It's his loss."

"Yeah," Bobbi agreed.

Soon all the girls were offering her words of comfort, although she hadn't confirmed she'd been dumped.

Well, all the girls except Ariel, who was still staring at some imaginary spot on her desk.

Eli got the class back under control and started her day's lesson plan. The class flew by. When the bell rang again, the girls immediately started gathering their belongings. Ariel practically sprang from her desk and sprinted toward the door.

"Ariel, could I see you for a minute?" Eli called.

Ariel froze, and with apparent reluctance, turned around and walked back to Eli's desk, her head down.

"Mel, would you close the door after you?" she called to the straggler.

Eli waited until the door was shut. "Ariel, what's wrong?"

"Nothing."

She'd been a teacher too long not to know there was something very wrong here. "Is there something wrong with your baby?"

Ariel shook her head, and since she'd chosend another indistinct point to stare at, her blond hair flopped forward, hiding even her brow.

"Your aunt? Work? School?" Eli asked.

More head shaking.

"Ariel? Talk to me. I thought we were friends."

Ariel's head jerked up and she faced Eli, anger flashing in her eyes. "We weren't friends. We're not friends. You're just another stupid teacher, telling me what to do, and I'm just some dumb teenager who's screwed up her whole life by getting pregnant. You can't fix my life. Hell, you can't even fix your own life." And with that, Ariel stormed out of the classroom.

Eli sat at her desk, not sure what to do. Should she run after Ariel and apologize? For what? For getting pregnant and being dumped? For being human?

Somehow Eli made it until the end of the day. All she wanted to do was go home and hide. Hide from her life.

She opened the door to the silent house. The afternoons got dark early, so it felt gloomy, but she didn't turn on any lights. Instead, she went to her room, put on her oldest, most comfortable pair of sweats and her Mercyhurst College sweatshirt, made some herbal tea and sat at her desk, going over her plans for next week's mentor panel.

She made absolutely no headway. She aimlessly turned the pages of her notebook, and occasionally doodled in the margins, but her thoughts kept drifting back to Ariel.

She could rationalize Ariel's reaction. Ariel had lost everything she knew when she'd become pregnant. Her parents had kicked her out, her boyfriend had left her and she couldn't be on the cheerleading squad in her condition. She was mad. And in her mind, Eli had now let her down, as well, and in so doing had become a perfect target for some of that anger.

Eli had spent her entire teaching career trying to be a good example to her students, but while *she* knew good example didn't equal perfect, maybe Ariel had missed that bulletin.

Well, that was fine, because Eli wasn't exactly thrilled about her circumstances, either. She'd never planned on being in her forties, pregnant and alone. Yet, here she was. She looked down and what had started out to be a doodle had become an angry knot of scribbles.

She balled up the piece of paper and threw it at the garbage can…and missed.

Perfect. Just perfect. She'd made a mess of her life, her career and now she was making a mess in her house. She got up and picked the paper up and placed it in the can.

The doorbell rang. She couldn't imagine who it was, but truth be told she hoped it was someone trying to sell something—someone she'd be able to dismiss quickly. She opened the door to find Zac on the porch. "Oh, it's you."

"Wow." He was seemingly unphased by her lack of enthusiasm, as he walked past her into the house.

She shut the door, resigned to the fact she had a guest, like it or not.

"I thought we'd moved beyond such effusive displays of delight." He smiled, as if he could jolly her out of her funk. She noticed that his grins were so broad that they made the skin around his eyes crinkle. It was as if Zac's entire face took the business of smiling seriously.

He removed his coat and boots, and headed straight for her living room. Over the last month, he'd become quite at home at her house. "Uh, a bit dark, isn't it?" The only light in the room was coming through the window.

"Maybe I'm in a dark mood."

He clicked on the floorlamp next to the couch, sat down and indicated she should sit beside him. "Okay, so, what happened today to put you in a dark mood? Because Eli, you're the least dark person I know."

She sat, not because she was obeying him, but because she was pregnant and she should probably sit. "Nothing happened."

"Liar." When she didn't respond, he asked, "Want me to call Tuck for you? I mean, I know you two have been friends longer than we have. It won't hurt my feelings. If you can't talk to me, talk to her."

There was a tightness at the back of her throat that made it impossible to say anything. She literally couldn't seem to push the words past that point.

"Here, let me call her."

"No" was all she managed to get out before the tightness became a rush of tears. Not some little moisture leaking from her eyes, but a full gush.

"Hey, hey," Zac said and without asking, without waiting, he simply pulled her into his arms.

She started to pull away, but he held tight. Not in an uncomfortable way, but rather he held on in the way that only a good friend would know how to do.

She leaned on his shoulder and continued crying as he patted her back and murmured a string of there-theres, I'm-heres and it's-all-going-to-be-okays.

"But it's not," she finally managed to reply, her head still buried in his now soggy shoulder.

"Can you explain?"

She nodded and lifted her chin from his shoulder. She felt slightly deflated after her hysterics. Deflated and embarrassed. "I'm so sorry. That's so not like me."

"Eli, a few tears can't scare me off. And I know it's not like you, so I know something's happened. I meant what I said, if you can't tell me, I'll call Tucker, or your mom, even if she's in Florida, she's just a phone call away. Hell, even my mom. You have to talk to someone. I hate seeing you like this."

ZAC WANTED TO PUNCH someone. He just needed Eli to tell him who.

He liked to think of himself as a peaceful, easygoing guy, but right now, he had to crush whoever had upset her. He'd never felt such an overwhelming need to protect someone since the day the social worker came for Cessy.

He shut out the memory and concentrated on the here and now—on Eli's needs.

"It was just a very bad day," she said, softly.

"Is something wrong with the baby?"

"No. No, nothing like that. I mean, other than the fact I can't button my pants anymore. Since last week."

"And that's set you off? It's okay. You'll get back into them after the baby."

"No, no, I know I'll get back into them. And I'm not so vain that it freaked me out, but it did make me realize I couldn't put off telling people at school any longer. I mean, once you're wearing maternity clothes, the news is sort of out there."

"And it didn't go well?"

"The teachers, my colleagues, were supportive. Well, I really just told the ones I'm close with, and figure that the news would make it to the rest of them in record time. The principal was supportive as well. Of course, he asked if I'd be needing time off for the wedding."

"Subtle as a brick."

"No, it wasn't mean. He's met Arthur and assumed that we'd—" She cut herself off. "Anyway, I told him no, there was no wedding in the works. That Arthur was out of the picture. The principal's a nice guy, but he's a guy, and he got this look on his face that said he was afraid I'd start crying, but I didn't. He seemed relieved and told me congratulations and to let him know if I needed anything. I spent the day telling more people."

"And that's why you're crying? Someone else said something?" Again, the need to find whoever had made Eli cry was as overwhelming as it was a surprise. Chest thumping he-man was not Zac's normal M.O. but it was out in full force.

"No. All the teachers were great. And Doris, the secretary, jumped up and hugged me and swore she was going to get her knitting supplies out the minute she got home. Between her and my mom, this baby will have booties well into his or her forties. No, that all went well. It was later, when I told my students." She gave a little post-cry hiccup.

"They didn't take it well."

"Most of them did. It's just, Ariel didn't. I know that teachers aren't supposed to have favorites, and yet we're human and we do. I try to make sure I don't show her favoritism, but she reminds me so much of Tucker. You wouldn't think she would. I don't know if I ever mentioned that Tucker's real name is Angelina, but no one ever calls her that. It's too girly, she'd tell you off if you tried. And Ariel has always struck me as the personification of all things girly. So, on the surface, they're nothing alike, but inside, where it counts, they're very much the same."

"And you care."

"Probably more than I should. Tucker's dad was supportive after he adjusted, but she didn't have a mom to go to, and Ariel…well, I get the feeling her aunt is more about materially looking after her than emotionally.

Her aunt's sort of young, she's gone a lot and I don't think she knows what to do for Ariel. Tucker and Ariel…they both needed that maternal gap filled. And I tried."

"And when you told her, there was no support from her? She hurt you."

Eli shook her head. "I shouldn't let it get to me. I mean, I understand her reaction. She's a scared, angry teen, and I was a place for her to vent."

"After all you've done for her—"

"I did my job." Even though Eli'd stopped crying and was barely hiccuping any longer, he still pulled her back into his arms. He thought she'd protest, but she simply returned his embrace.

"El, what you do for Ariel—for all the girls—is so much more than your job."

She mumbled something against his chest, then simply went still, allowing him to comfort her. That was what all he wanted to do, and more.

She was obviously done talking. He could feel her relax in his arms, and for the longest time he just held her as he desperately tried to think of something, anything, to cheer her up.

"Hey, wanna go shopping this weekend?"

He could have shot himself for breaking the comfortable silence because Eli's head popped up off his shoulder.

"Is this a pity shop? See the pregnant woman cry and toss her a shopping bone?"

"No, this was a totally selfish request. I desperately need help buying Christmas presents for the ladies in the family. Dad and the boys are easy. I just buy them a subscription to *Sports Illustrated,* or something, and they're happy. But you can't just buy women magazine subscriptions. They get testy."

Sitting there wearing an old college sweatshirt, her face streaked from her tears, she smiled and looked utterly beautiful to him. "How can I say no? I mean, saving your mom and sisters from a magazine subscription is a worthy cause."

"Then it's a date."

"Zac, we've had this discussion." She scooted toward the end of the couch, putting as much distance as possible between them. "I just want to be clear."

"Eli, answer me this—do you like spending time with me?" He wasn't sure she was going to answer, but slowly she nodded her head. "And I like spending time with you.

So, what's the difference if we call it two friends going shopping together, or dating?"

"A world of difference, and you know it. Maybe we shouldn't go."

"Or maybe we should—" Zac was done. He'd been playing the nice guy since September. He'd been her buddy, her pal, and while he loved that, he wanted them to be a proper couple. So in a decisive, non-buddy, non-pal way he moved closer to her and kissed her. He didn't hold her, although he wanted to. He wouldn't force the kiss, but she didn't back up. If anything she deepened it. She made a small sound of pleasure in the back of her throat that was almost his undoing.

After months, Zac Keller was kissing Eli Cartwright the way he'd longed to since the day they'd met.

He could have gone on doing so for much longer, but slowly, he withdrew. "I think we could safely go shopping and call it a date."

"Zac, you're younger than me and I'm pregnant with another man's baby."

"I think there's a chance you're saying those things to remind yourself, more than remind me, why you're scared. I'm not scared by our age difference. I mean, you wouldn't think anything of it if I were the older one, would you?" She didn't answer. She didn't have to.

"So, that's a double standard, isn't it?" He added, "As for the baby, well, I'll admit, the timing's odd and we're not talking about forever, only a date, but Eli, the idea of a baby that's not mine isn't a deterrent, either. You know that my siblings and I are adopted, just looking at us, it's obvious. I learned a long time ago that being a family has everything to do with love."

At the word she frowned and sniffled some more.

"But we're not talking about love," he hastily assured her. "We're talking about a Christmas shopping date. I'll come pick you up, we'll head to Erie and the Millcreek Mall, and since it's a date, you'll let me take you to dinner afterward. I'll open doors for you, and hold your chair."

"What if we're sitting at a booth?" she asked softly.

Zac hadn't realized how tense he was, but as she teased him, he felt his neck and shoulder muscles release. She was going to say yes. "I'll take you someplace that has tables."

"This is probably not a good idea. We haven't even talked about the fact I'm on the rebound."

There were many things in life that Zac didn't know, and he was the first to admit them. But this one he knew with utter certainty—Eli wasn't on the rebound with Arthur. Whatever they had was over. "No, I think there's a month or so that's the rebound zone. And we were friends hanging out then. You're past that, so we can date without worrying."

She patted her small baby bump. "Not worrying?"

He leaned forward and gave her a small tender kiss on the cheek. "I'm not worried in the least."

"Zac, you're crazy."

About you was the response he'd have liked to give, but he'd taken this as far as he dared tonight. They were going on a date. That was enough progress for an evening. "Hey, have you met my family? I'm the sane one."

She gave him a more convincing smile. "Yes, I have met them and they're quite sane."

"Oh, come on, you're just being nice. They're nuts."

"You're nuts about them."

"Guilty." And because she seemed to be feeling better and he was feeling daring, he went ahead and added, "And I'm nuts about you."

She gave him a tsk tsk. "What am I going to do about you?"

"Right now, you're going to follow me into the kitchen, where I'm going to check your refrigerator and find something to feed you. Then, I'm challenging you to a brisk game of Scrabble. I saw the box in the closet."

"Feed me first?"

"Hey, when I totally trounce you, I don't want you crying because you were at a disadvantage because you were hungry."

"As if you'll beat me. My mom and Tucker refuse to play with me because I win a lot. And by a lot I mean, most of the time."

"How about your dad?" he asked, as he walked toward the kitchen with her trailing after him.

"Who do you think taught me how to play? Our games were cutthroat."

"Well, we'll have to see how we match up." He was pretty sure they'd be a good match, win, lose or draw.

THE NEXT DAY, ZAC CHECKED Ariel's schedule and was waiting in the employee's room when she clocked in. "How's it going, Ariel?"

Ariel looked nervous. "Fine, Mr. Keller."

She hurried to her locker and stowed her coat and purse, and pulled out her cashier's smock. Carefully buttoning it over her swollen stomach, she turned and saw him waiting. "Really, everything's fine. I love working here."

But it wasn't fine. He could tell. "And you? Are you okay?"

"Sure. How about you? I hear congratulations are in order." There was a hardness in her tone.

He didn't confirm or deny he was Eli's baby's father. He just said quietly, "Whatever there is between Ms. Cartwright and me is our business, Ariel."

"Sure, yours and the baby's. That's what Ms. Cartwright always says, that it takes two people to make a baby and both are responsible for it." She snorted. "Sometimes the guys don't get her classroom notes on the subject though."

"There are similarities between your situation and Ms. Cartwright's, but there's one major difference. She's an adult. A self-sup-

porting adult who knows what she wants."
He paused and asked gently, "Why does this
bother you so much?"

"Why?" Ariel kicked her locker door shut.
"'Cause there she is, Ms. Cartwright, a
teacher who knows about this stuff. And still,
she makes a mistake—"

"Did she say the baby was a mistake?" he
asked pointedly.

Ariel shook her head.

"Well, why would you assume it is?"

"I—"

"Listen, I'm not sure why you're so mad
at her. And I don't want to get in the middle
of it. I will say, however, that you hurt her.
And though I know Ms. Cartwright doesn't
play favorites, you're special to her. I don't
know how you couldn't know that."

He walked out of the room without looking back.

He knew that Eli wouldn't appreciate his
interfering, but he couldn't stand to see her
cry as she had last night. And if he were
honest, he had to admit, it wasn't only Eli, it
was Ariel. He'd grown close to the girl, and
knew that she needed Eli.

Maybe his words would make a difference.

THAT FRIDAY, ELI BUSTLED around the classroom, setting up for the day's panel discussion. Three of her former teen-parenting students were coming in to talk to the current students and serve as role models. Mentors.

Tucker had agreed to participate, although it took a lot of arm-twisting and laying on the guilt.

She was the first one to show up. "I'm here. I even put on semi-grown-up clothes, and you know how I hate that."

Rather than her normal paint-splattered jeans and T-shirt, she had on a pair of dark brown slacks and a navy sweater. She'd taken her hair out of its quintessential ponytail and soft curls framed her face.

Sometimes Eli forgot how beautiful Tucker was.

"Tucker, it's time like these that I know you care."

Tucker missed the teasing in Eli's voice and simply nodded. "And I even put on makeup. Not a lot, but some. I hate that, too."

Eli laughed. "You're a good friend."

Tucker laughed as well. "Yes, I am. Still, you're going to have to make it up to me.

Maybe we should go out to dinner and a show on Saturday."

Eli was about to say yes, when she remembered she'd agreed to go out with Zac. "Maybe Sunday?" she countered.

Tucker plopped into one of the chairs Eli had set up at the front of the room. "Come here and sit. What's up on Saturday? You have a look, Eli."

Eli ignored Tucker's invitation to sit and went to her desk instead. She knew why she was reluctant to tell Tucker. If she said the words, it would make the date real. Instead, she simply replied, "Nothing's up. I just have plans."

"What kind of plans? Plans that center around a certain grocery store owner?"

Eli busied herself with a stack of papers, trying to ignore Tucker's question.

Tucker, however, was a force of nature—impossible to ignore. She sprang out of the chair and hurried next to Eli at the desk, putting herself directly in Eli's line of sight. "A date? You finally broke down and are going on a date with him?"

"It's Christmas shopping." She took the pile of papers and moved it to her file cabinet. "And maybe dinner."

Tucker followed her. "That sounds like a date."

"Don't get too excited." She dumped the papers into an empty file at the front of the drawer because she had no idea what they were and where they actually belonged, and this way, later, she could find them easily.

She practically tripped over Tucker, who was directly behind her. "Seriously, Tuck, it's nothing major."

"I like him a lot more than I liked Arthur. Of course, you know that's not saying much, so let's say that I really like Zac, and I like who you are when you're with him."

Eli wanted to ask what Tucker meant by that last line, but didn't because she also wasn't sure she wanted to hear what Tucker had to say. "Arthur and I were compatible, though. Zac and I? There are a lot of strikes against us."

"Like what?" Tucker took her by the hand, led her to the chairs, sat in one and gently pulled Eli into the other. "Tell me."

It took Eli a moment to remember her own arguments. "His age…my age."

"Huh?"

"He's younger. And I'm pregnant…let's not forget that. Pregnant with another man's child. Those are two big hurdles."

Tucker shrugged. "I still think he's better than Arthur. And if Arthur's an example of compatible, then maybe it's time to think about something different."

They didn't get any further with the discussion since Greg and Deborah, her former students, came in. Hugs were exchanged and they all caught up for a few moments.

Eli didn't miss the fact that Tucker was giving her a look. And she knew what it was saying. Coward. Tucker thought Eli was simply avoiding getting hurt with all her excuses about Zac.

And maybe she was, but that wasn't necessarily cowardly, it was being careful.

The students arrived on the heels of her guests, and after the obligatory minutes of shuffling and settling in, Eli started.

"As I told you yesterday, we're going to hear from guest speakers today. They'll each take turns telling you a bit about their experience as teen parents, and what they're doing now. When they're done, they'll take questions from you. We'll start with Angelina Tucker." Tucker grimaced as Eli used her first name. "She's the reason this program exists today. It was almost sixteen years ago that Tucker came to me for help when she found out that she was pregnant. There were no programs in the district to assist girls in her situation and—"

Tucker interrupted Eli's introduction. "And you all know Ms. Cartwright. When she found out there was nothing out there to help me, she just helped me herself."

The girls all laughed.

Eli continued. "Today, Ms. Tucker's a successful graphic artist. She specializes in motorcycles, and there are people all over the country who want a bike that Tucker's worked on. Tucker, why don't you take it from here?"

"Hi, everyone. Let's just forget that Ms. Cartwright mentioned my first name. I'm Tucker. Not Ms. Tucker, Miss Tucker, or Mrs. Tucker. Just Tucker. And before someone raises their hand to tell me you have to call me something formal, I'll save you the effort, I'm not a teacher, so you don't."

The girls all laughed, and Eli smiled. She'd had Tucker come in for years, and it always went this way. Tucker had an instant connection with the girls that stemmed from the fact she was genuine. There was no artifice in her, and the girls responded to that.

"And it doesn't seem like that long ago I

was a student here. A pregnant student. My boyfriend wanted nothing to do with a baby, and he'd made that perfectly clear. My mother was dead, I didn't have any aunts or sister, so I came to Ms. Cartwright. She came with me when I told me father. I figured he'd do me in, but my dad, well, he was great. He's been my son's father figure. But he didn't know much about pregnancy or babies. It was Ms. Cartwright who got me prepared, who came with me to childbirth classes…."

Eli could feel her cheeks warming as Tucker continued on her Eli-fest. She didn't know how to stop it. Tucker made it all sound so much more than it was. She hadn't done anything special. She'd just helped a student. That was her job.

She glanced at Ariel in the back row. She'd purposely avoided Eli ever since Eli had announced her pregnancy. She didn't know what to do about Ariel. Maybe there was nothing she could do. Maybe she shouldn't even try.

She was Ariel's teacher. She'd done her job—was doing her job. That she'd somehow failed to live up to Ariel's expectations wasn't her fault.

Tucker finished and Eli got up and introduced Greg Warton, a local disc jockey who'd been her first teen dad through the program. "Okay, I know you all know this, but teen parents aren't just teen moms. My girlfriend and I…"

There were currently no boys in the program, despite the fact Eli actively recruited. Maybe if she found a male teacher…

She introduced their third panelist, Julie, and when she finished, Eli said, "I'm sure you all have questions. Please raise your hands and remember to be polite."

Forty-five minutes later, the class ended. She ushered the kids out and thanked all her panelists.

Tucker was the last to leave. "You okay?"

"Sure."

"So, you'll call after your date with Zac and we'll go out on Sunday?"

"I wish you wouldn't call it that." Date. She knew she'd agreed, but the word weighed heavily on her.

"Is that what he's calling it?" Tucker persisted.

She remembered his kiss and nodded.

"Then maybe you should get used to calling it that, too." Tucker paused and said, "Date. Date. Date. Come on, Eli. You can do it."

"Date." She tried to sound put out, but with Tucker standing there grinning at her, it was impossible. She suspected she even had a hint of a smile on her face. "Date. I've said it. Are you happy?"

"Getting happier," Tucker admitted. "So, what are you going to wear?"

"Oh, man, you know things are bad when Angelina Tucker starts asking me about my wardrobe. To answer your question, I'm going to wear whatever fits."

"That bad?"

Eli lifted her top and revealed the rubber band that connected her pants button to the button hole. It was a stopgap measure at best. "I think it's time to admit that I need maternity clothes."

"Well, we could go shopping." Tucker's offer was made with obvious reluctance. "I remember I had this great teacher who took me out and helped me buy a few necessities when I no longer fit in my clothes."

"And I remember I had this student who decided maternity clothes were horrible and spent the last five months of her pregnancy wearing sweatpants and her father's flannel shirts and T-shirts."

"I bet I could borrow some of his stuff for

you, too. Although, they might not be the most professional outfits for a teacher."

"Thanks. And thank your dad, even though he didn't make the offer. But I'll probably have to break down and buy some maternity clothes soon."

"Okay, so call me and we'll skip the movie and just do the maternity store and lunch."

"Shopping for clothes is your idea of torture."

"Yeah, but I like you enough to suffer for our friendship."

"It's a date."

"See, you can use the word without grimacing." Tucker started for the door. "Call me after that other big date."

"I'll call you, all right…." Eli was talking to the door.

What was she doing? Single, pregnant and dating a younger man?

CHAPTER SEVEN

"Maternity clothes. Some women love them. Some hate them. But as your waistline expands, they become a necessity. Today's trends are much more fashion friendly."
—*Pregnancy, Childbirth and Parenting for Teens,* by Mary Jeanne Lorei

THE NEXT DAY, ZAC found a parking space... way at the back end of the lot. He was glad he'd dropped Eli off at the door to the mall. She'd protested that she was perfectly capable of walking, but he'd simply pulled over next to the entrance and waited until she got out. She'd grumbled as she did.

He smiled as he waded through the three or so inches of snow that had fallen since the plows had been through.

It might not be officially winter until the end of December, but in Western Pennsylvania, winter could arrive anytime after Halloween—sometimes before. It was still early enough in December that this current batch of snow would probably melt, but it would be sticking around soon enough.

Thinking about snow was easier than worrying about what was his first official date with Eli. It wasn't what he'd have chosen, but Eli was still tepid, to say the least, about dating him. Although she didn't seem all that tepid about him personally. As a matter of fact, their kiss was pretty hot.

That thought warmed him as he hurried toward the mall.

Eli was stubbornly standing outside the Sears door waiting for him. "Why didn't you go inside where it's warm?"

"You know, Zac, scolding a woman isn't the best way to start a date."

Before he could respond, she continued, "And I was outside because I like the snow. I like watching the hustle and bustle here, especially this time of year." She dug in her pocket and stuffed a bill into the Salvation Army kettle as they walked by it. "I just love the season."

That didn't surprise him in the least. "So, where do we start?" he asked as they stood in

the concourse. Zac knew it fed into stereo-
types, but he couldn't help it. He hated
shopping.

"You need to get things for your sisters
and mom?"

He nodded.

"Do you have a guideline money-wise?"

He gave her his figure.

She smiled. "Oh, this is almost too easy.
Let's go."

Eli was an organized, no-nonsense
shopper. That didn't surprise him. They had
a very pretty locket for his mom within the
first half hour and then headed toward one of
the trendy teen stores to find something for
Cessy.

"So, how did your panel go yesterday?" he
asked as they strolled down the concourse.

"Fine. I started the role-model panel my
second year with the program. We didn't
have any real graduates, so I found former
teen parents throughout the community.
They were wonderful and the kids enjoyed
them, but it's so much more rewarding to
see the kids you worked so hard with come
back as success stories. Tucker came in.
She's always a great role model for the kids.
She has an ability to really reach them."

He heard the word she wasn't saying, so he supplied it. "But?"

She stopped in front of a candy cane pole at the Santa Claus station. Her frown contrasted with the smiles on everyone else's faces. "But what?"

"There was a 'but' in there," he insisted. "Remember what Cessy pointed out. I can hear you even when you're not talking." He looked up and saw a sprig of mistletoe hanging off the pole. He didn't mention how much he'd like to indulge in the age-old custom. No, he simply waited for her to tell him just what the *but* was.

Eli's silence was broken when she sighed. "*But* even Tucker couldn't reach Ariel…at least not on my behalf."

"She's still upset?"

Eli shrugged and looked disheartened. "I can only assume, since she's not talking to me. Oh, she'll answer if called on in class, but otherwise, nothing."

Eli started walking down the concourse again. Santa had a line of kids waiting to see him, and there was a holiday train running around in circles behind him. Its merry whistle seemed to punctuate Eli's words.

Wanting to comfort her, and knowing it

was risky, Zac took her hand in his. "Want me to talk to her?" He hadn't really talked to her before, he'd simply mentioned that Eli was upset. This time he'd be more firm.

Eli didn't withdraw her hand from his. As a matter of fact, she gave his hand a firm squeeze. "No. But thanks. Like I said, she needs a target and I'm convenient."

"How is everyone else reacting?"

"Fine. Better than fine. The other teachers are great, and Lainey came up to me the other day and said that she always liked my class, but now she really knows I get it because Arthur dumped me like her boyfriend dumped her." She paused. "You know, I've always done everything I can to reach the girls. I don't know why I never gave this approach a try before now."

She was trying to make a joke, but it fell flat.

"Eli, it'll all be okay." He paused and asked, "So have you heard from Arthur lately?"

"Not since that last time. I want him to give me the parental termination papers and just step away. I don't like ambiguity."

"It will work out." It made him feel like a schmuck, but truth be told he was relieved she hadn't heard from Arthur. If he really thought Arthur was the man to make Eli happy, he'd have tracked the guy down himself. But he didn't think Arthur was the man for Eli. Zac very much believed he was. "Really, it will all end up the way it was meant to be."

"Most days I believe that. Sometimes, though, it's harder." She hesitated and then added in a blatant attempt to change the conversation, "But Zac Keller, I didn't think you were the kind of guy who believed in destiny."

"We all grew up listening to Mom talk about how we were all meant to be a family. That it was destiny. So I've always believed in it." He squeezed her hand. "And sometimes I believe in it a lot."

She looked away, and he knew he'd come on too strong, too fast.

When she continued looking at the other side of the mall, he knew it wasn't just that he'd made her uncomfortable. Zac turned and saw she was checking out a maternity store. "Want to go in?"

"No, that's fine. Tucker offered to come with me to shop for clothes."

"I take it from your expression that she doesn't enjoy shopping."

"You hardly know her, and yet you know her so well. I'll confess, I'm no window-shopper. I tend to come into a store or mall, get what I need, then get out. But Tuck's barely stepped foot in any store other than a grocery store, and most of the time, her dad does their grocery shopping. No, her offer was a firm sign of how deep her friendship goes. Besides, I can't imagine going into a maternity store is any more your cup of tea than hers."

"Well, the good news is, Tucker will owe me one. And I'm guessing she's a very good person to have in your corner. Come on. If you can help me shop for my mom and sisters, the least I can do is go with you to look around a maternity store since we're here."

"I do need some pants. Desperately."

"Then, let's go." Zac liked to think of himself as a brave man, but walking into the maternity store with Eli was one of the bravest things he'd done in a while.

One of the saleswomen approached them before they'd taken more than two steps inside. Soon thereafter she led Eli off. There was a seating area in the back, so Zac sat, content to wait. He noticed a book on a nearby table. *What Every Father Should Know.* He picked it up and thumbed through it. Chapters titled "What To Do When She's Breastfeeding" and "Emotional Roller Coasters." *"Remember, that while your role might not be as obvious as the mother's, babies need a father's care. Boy or girl, they need a male role model...."*

Eli's baby would need a male role model. Would Zac be around long enough to be it?

He glanced at Eli as Eli had worn a bulky sweater under her coat, but when she moved the right way, her stomach's small bulge was evident. He noticed her hand rested lightly on it, as if the baby inside were her touchstone, something she needed to reassure herself was still there.

It was too soon to talk about being there for this baby, in his heart he already was. He'd have no trouble being a father. He couldn't help but think of his parents and siblings. No, he didn't need to be related to this baby genetically in order to parent it. He wasn't sure Eli got that yet.

"Being Daddy is More Than Just Tossing Around a Football," a chapter in the book proclaimed.

He thought of his father. Abe Keller hadn't been much on tossing footballs, but he'd been there in so many ways. School plays,

PTA meetings. His dad had even been one of the chaperones on an overnight trip to Cleveland when Zac was in eighth grade. He hadn't thought anything of it at the time, but later he realized that being trapped in a hotel room with four boys might not have been his father's idea of a good time.

No, there might not be any shared DNA between them, but Abe Keller was a great father and a real role model for what a dad should be.

Zac wanted nothing less for Eli's baby. And he didn't think Arthur came close to stacking up. The man was…

He forced himself not to think about Arthur.

That's not what Eli needed. She needed a friend. She needed support.

And he hoped she was beginning to need him.

She appeared with a stack of clothing in her arms. "I'm going to try a few things on, if you're sure you don't mind."

He held the book up. "I'm reading. Take your time."

He watched her walk toward the changing room. She had a bit of a waddle because of the large stack of clothing. Soon she'd be waddling because of the ever expanding girth of her stomach. She'd be cute.

He turned back to the book and flipped to another chapter. "Adoptive Fathers."

"Being a father is more than biology. Parents aren't tied to their children by blood, but rather by love. Remember that. Your baby needs you. Your wife needs you...."

The chapter echoed so many things his parents had taught him.

"Good book?"

Zac looked up and saw Eli standing in front of him, two big bags in hand.

"Wow, that was fast." He set down the book, got up and took the bags before she could protest. "You obviously got some shopping done."

"Yes." She turned shy. "And I know this wasn't exactly the best first date ever, I mean, it's different all right. Sitting around a maternity store while your date shops."

"Eli, you don't get it yet, do you?" he asked as they left the maternity store.

She stopped to the side of the entryway and studied him. "Get what, Zac?"

He set down the bags containing her maternity clothes and his Christmas presents. "I don't care what we do, I just like being with you. Whether we're talking about the CATA Project, watching a basketball game or shopping—I like it because you're there, too."

"You're right, I don't get it. I'm pregnant. I'm getting fatter by the minute and…" She looked truly confused. "I just don't get it. I'm nothing special."

"Now, there's a subject for a great debate because I disagree."

He'd given Eli's hang-ups about dating him some serious thought. It was time to lay it all on the line.

He didn't need any special insight to see that she was going to be a tough sell.

"Let me ask you something."

"Okay."

"Don't look so worried. It's not about you and me, it's about Tucker. I take it she dates on occasion?"

Eli appeared confused. "Very rarely, but yes, she dates."

"And she has a kid?" he asked.

Eli nodded.

"And it doesn't bother you that she dates?"

He saw the lightbulb moment, when she understood where his questions were going. "Zac—"

"Come on, Eli, just so we're clear. You

don't have any fundamental problem with the idea of single moms dating, right?"

"You're right, I don't have problems with single moms dating. But I'm not quite a mom yet, I'm a mom-to-be. And may I point out, I agreed to a date."

"You reluctantly agreed to a date. If I were a less confident man, I'd have been wounded by the extreme coercion I've had to exert to get you to agree. Now, what you're saying is that if I'd been willing to wait until after you had the baby, you'd have been more comfortable with the idea of dating me?"

"When you put it that way, my reluctance sounds stupid. It's not the pregnancy alone. It's the fact you're younger." She stared at him stubbornly.

He wasn't buying it. "I'm not younger by that much."

She snorted. "I could have practically babysat you."

"No, you couldn't have. I'm pretty sure I read an article about the fact Pennsylvania doesn't have a law on the books about what is old enough to babysit, but it said eleven was considered old enough by the courts. And I know my mom never let us babysit until we were twelve. So, no, you couldn't have babysat me."

"Almost," she insisted.

"It's sort of a double standard, isn't it? I mean, if a girl was dating a guy who was older, you wouldn't think anything about it."

"I don't know—"

"And given that women statistically live longer than men, it really makes more sense for women to date younger guys."

She smiled.

It was the smallest upturn of her lips, but it was indeed the beginning of a smile.

"Zac—"

"Lastly, let me simply point out that when you're past your twenties, a few years doesn't really represent any huge life-experience gap. For instance, what do you listen to in the car?"

There was no hinting now, Eli wore a full-out smile. He could sense she was weakening.

"Country," she admitted.

"There you go. I love country. Rascal Flatts, Taylor Swift, Carrie Underwood. I'll confess, I watch *American Idol* and liked her even then."

"Me, too. I love it."

"Well, there you go. We watch the same shows, and can talk the same music language. So, what it comes down to is—do you like me? I feel like I'm back in school, but still I'll ask, if you weren't pregnant, and if my age wasn't a factor, would you like me enough to date me?"

"And if I hadn't just gotten out of a long-term relationship."

He'd won. He knew it. He wasn't going to gloat, but if that was the last of her arguments, then Zac knew he'd won. "No, that one doesn't count. Whatever we have growing between us is absolutely not a rebound relationship. We waited quite a while before today's first date, so no. You don't get to use that argument, either." He grinned to let her know he was teasing.

"It seems I'm not winning any argument today." Eli went from smiling to out and out laughing.

"So, we're an item? Dating?"

She shook her head. "You're crazy and beyond persistent."

"Your answer?"

"Fine, so we're dating."

"That wasn't so hard, was it?" It was a huge hurdle. Zac felt like celebrating.

The holiday crowd was bustling around them, and he purposefully turned the conversation to something lighter. "So, how long are you off for the holidays?"

SOMEWHERE DURING HIS reflections on dating, Eli had admitted to herself her real reason for not wanting to date Zac—she was afraid. Arthur had been comfortable. Easy, even. They both maintained their own homes, their own spaces. They didn't mingle at each other's jobs. They were together regularly, but neither had ever done much calling on days they didn't see each other.

Now, here was Zac, and nothing about him was easy. He'd found a way into her life and sort of filled in all the cracks and rounded off the edges. He called every day until one day she realized she was waiting for his call. Looking forward to it, even. And she saw him all the time. There was no regularity about it. He was simply with her whenever possible.

She'd met his family and had a standing invitation to weekend dinners. They'd even included Tucker. It took two years before she'd met Arthur's sister, and even after that, when Ashley came to town Arthur was apt to see her on his own.

"There's a Christmas party coming up for the Keller's Markets' employees. Want to go?"

"You're sure you want to introduce me to the people you work with? I mean, I'm more and more pregnant with each passing day and they're bound to speculate…."

"I don't care what people think. I've liked you for a very long time. There was an instant attraction when I met you, but as I got to know you it went beyond that. The only thing that kept me from actively pursuing you was that you were in a relationship and seemed happy. And I grew to care about you too much to do anything that would dim that happiness." He paused and added, "And I don't poach. I've never poached. You were the one case where I was tempted. But now you're not in a relationship, and I'm not in a relationship. So, we'll go out."

"And if people talk?" she asked.

"People always talk, Eli. When Mom and Dad adopted us, they talked."

His response confused her. "About?"

"About the fact they had kids of mixed races. Or when they adopted someone like me, who was older, people worried that I'd be a bad seed. When Mom and Dad adopted more than three kids, they talked about the fact they were crazy…they were getting older and would never be able to handle a big family. People talked then, Eli. Odds are they'll talk now. That kind of talk seems to be a part of the human condition. But I don't care. Do you?"

She knew that if she and Zac got any more deeply involved there were bound to be hurdles.

As much as she knew that maybe she should care, the truth was, she didn't care at all.

She took his hand in hers. It felt solid. It felt right. "No, I don't care what anyone says."

Eli had spent months feeling a bit crazed by all the unexpected changes in her life. She was someone who liked to have things planned out. And yet, here she was inviting another change…and rather than finding that daunting, she couldn't seem to stop smiling.

For the first time in months, she felt like she was getting something right.

CHAPTER EIGHT

"A new baby is a gift. Sometimes, when circumstances aren't ideal, it's hard to remember that, but in every baby there's a sense of potential, a dream for the future…and that is a gift, regardless of the circumstances."

—*Pregnancy, Childbirth and Parenting for Teens,* by Mary Jeanne Lorei

"JINGLE BELLS, JINGLE BELLS…" Eli sang giddily.

Zac laughed. "Someone's got the Christmas spirit."

"Everyone was so nice at your work party. I'd been worried."

"I told you not to be."

"You might not have noticed, but I don't *always* listen," she said cheekily. She hung up their coats and walked toward the kitchen, but stopped in the doorway and turned to face him.

Zac was forced to stop, too. "Problem?"

Eli pointed at the ceiling. "The only problem is a boyfriend who neglects to follow tradition."

Zac looked up and a slow grin spread across his wind-chapped cheeks. "Why, Ms. Cartwright, what could that greenery be?"

"I suspect it's mistletoe, Mr. Keller. What do you suppose we should do about it?"

Zac didn't need a second invitation. He pulled her into his arms and kissed her which was just what she wanted.

Eli had discovered that kissing Zac was addictive.

It hadn't gone any further than kissing, and while part of her wanted it to, the other part—the part that needed to take this slow—was relieved that it hadn't. She moved her hands along the contour of Zac's back, loving the feel of him. Wanting to be closer…

The doorbell rang, interrupting both her thoughts and the kiss.

"Argh" was her not quite verbal response to the interruption.

"Argh?" Zac teased, though he sounded equally breathless. "I think I'm flattered."

"You should be." The doorbell rang again. "Who do you suppose that could be?"

"Tucker and Bart? Or maybe your parents?"

"They're on a cruise, so I doubt it." Eli hoped beyond hope that it was Tucker, who was a good enough friend not to take offense if Eli asked her to make the visit a short one.

"Merry Christmas," Eli cried as she opened the door. "Oh."

Arthur. To say he was the last person she expected to see would be a lie, but to say he was one of the last people she wanted to see was pretty much a given.

"Merry Christmas, Eli."

She stood there, not saying anything, not opening the door any farther.

Arthur.

Her silence and immobility must have gone on too long, because he finally asked, "May I come in?"

She let him into the entryway, glancing at Zac. "Sorry. This shouldn't take long."

"Don't worry. I'll go start the water for tea." He went into the kitchen.

"He's here?" Arthur asked.

She looked at her ex, who seemed none too pleased to find Zac at her house. "He's a friend. Now, what did you want, Arthur? Did you bring me the papers?"

"No. Could we go into the living room and sit down?"

"No, I don't think there's a need. Just tell me what you came here to say. I have company to get back to."

"I saw the lawyer and he's drawn up the papers to terminate my parental rights, as well as set up a trust fund for the—" he stumbled on the word "—baby."

"Great. Get back to me when they're signed." Eli felt a twinge of regret that it had come to this.

"That's just it." He stood ramrod-straight, his shoulders squared as he added, "I went down to sign them yesterday, and I couldn't do it." He looked as if he expected a fight.

Fighting wasn't what Eli had in mind, it never had been. "Are you saying you're planning to take a role in the baby's life?"

She was torn between believing that her baby had a right to know its father, and the knowledge that her life without Arthur in it was easier. What kind of mother would that make her? Putting her comfort over what was good for the baby?

"Is that what you're saying?" she repeated.

The unflappable college professor slumped a little and leaned against the wall, as if in need of support. "No. Yes. Maybe. I don't know. I just don't know, Eli. I'm so confused. I never wanted a…baby. And yet…" He shrugged.

She was tired of his waffling.

"I don't know how to help you with that, Arthur. To be honest, I've been confused. Having a baby in my forties wasn't what I expected, either. I had a life planned. Everything laid out. This wasn't a part of it."

"I know. I'm making a mess of all of this. I want to be a good guy, the kind who would stand by you in something like this, but every time I resolve to do just that, I see a kid or a baby and they're messy, demanding and…"

"And messy and demanding has never been something you've dealt with well. That's why I was a perfect girlfriend. I never asked for more than you could give. Our relationship was orderly. Dinners Friday nights. Something Saturday or Sunday afternoon. A standing date for the phil. I don't want to make it sound like this was all your fault. Let's face it, I was content with the status quo. It was easy for us, Arthur. But this isn't easy."

"No. No, it's not. And I miss you, Eli."

She realized he wasn't calling her Elinore anymore. Was he trying to please her?

"I loved knowing on Fridays we'd go out to dinner, or planning something for the weekend. I loved knowing that I had someone to go to the philharmonic with me. We were good together."

Eli realized that when he rattled off the things he loved, he never mentioned loving her—and she hadn't mentioned it, either. She didn't love him. And at this moment she knew with utter certainty that he had never loved her. "I can't help you decide what to do. Being part of the baby's life because you feel you have to, because you'd be able to think of yourself as a good guy, isn't enough." She heard herself start to lecture him and stopped. It wouldn't do anyone any good. "Listen, figure out what you want to do about the baby, then let me know."

She started to open the door, but Arthur put his hand on top of hers. "I truly miss you, El."

She wasn't sure what to say, so she simply slipped her hand out from under his.

"Please…"

"Arthur, you and I, we're over. I've told you. It's not a question you need to consider. That one's been answered. All that's left is for you to decide what you're going to do about the baby."

Arthur hit her doorjamb with his fist. "I don't know, damn it. I didn't ask for this."

"No, you didn't, neither did I. And yet, here we are."

As if that outburst had used up his energy, his shoulders slumped again. "I didn't come here to fight. I just missed you and wanted to wish you a merry Christmas."

"You, too, Arthur."

As he stepped away, he suddenly looked older than someone in his mid-fifties.

Eli watched until he got into his car before slowly closing her front door. Then she leaned into it, her face pressed to the winter-cold glass.

A sense of emptiness swept over her. She couldn't have really said why. She'd spent five years of her life with Arthur. And realized anew why it had been so easy to let him go: she had never loved him.

ZAC HELD ELI FOR A WHILE, enjoying the feeling of having his arm around her shoulder. Her arms were wrapped around her stomach, as if trying to protect the baby from a world where its own father didn't want it. Zac took his free hand and rested it on top of hers. Instantly, her being pregnant became real to him for the first time. He felt a sense of protectiveness—he'd do anything to save this child even one tear, one hurt feeling.

This wasn't his baby, but as his hand stayed on Eli's hands and stomach, that didn't matter. He loved this child sight unseen.

A baby who would need to be cherished… to be loved.

Arthur might not be sure if he could do it, but Zac knew in his heart that he already did. Completely.

And thoughts of losing the baby hurt as much as the thought of losing Eli.

The man had deserted both Eli and the baby. In Zac's book, that meant Arthur had forfeited his rights. Zac didn't see a way to make her understand that.

"Thanks for holding me," Eli said as she stirred. "You're a good man, Zac."

Her compliment embarrassed him, given that a more noble man, a better man, would be more understanding of her conflicted feelings about Arthur.

Zac thought a distraction might help. "We were going to deliver the baskets to Keller's employees tonight. Are you still feeling up to it?"

"I wouldn't miss it for the world."

"Well, bundle up and let's go."

Zac always volunteered to take holiday baskets to the employees, even when his dad still ran the markets. Zac enjoyed trying to sneak up to the employee's home and leave the basket without getting caught.

This year, he'd borrowed one of the store's trucks and had it loaded with the baskets. For three hours he and Eli made their way through Whedon, making deliveries to Zac's staff. Eli wanted to be the one to do the running, but he worried that she'd slip and fall on the snow-covered sidewalks, so he convinced her to be the driver.

She took the role to heart and sped away from each scene like a bank robber making her getaway, laughing with delight each time.

Zac could have stayed like this forever—just driving around town with Eli and listening to the sound of her delight.

But all too soon, there was only one basket remaining. "It's Ariel's," he told Eli. It was bigger than anyone else's because so many of the employees had come to him and asked him to include something they'd bought Ariel or the baby.

"That's not a basket, that's a crate," Eli said, smiling.

"Are things any better between the two of you?"

"No, not really. But I understand her, Zac. It's not my situation that's truly upset her. Ariel feels powerless, deserted even. And she's not just mad, she's pissed. Yes, her aunt's taking care of her, but her parents and boyfriend are gone. She's pissed at me, because deep down she trusts me. She trusts that I'll still care. I'm it, and though it stings a bit, I get it."

While Zac knew she meant every word she said, he also knew she was still hurt, and he wished he could do more to spare her that.

They pulled up in front of Ariel's aunt's place. He started to open the door, but Eli said, "Hang on a minute."

She dug through her purse that sat on the floor of the truck, and pulled out a beautifully wrapped gift. "Would you include this, please?"

He didn't ask what was inside, but simply took the small box and said, "Sure."

He went to the back of the truck, took out Ariel's "basket" and tucked Eli's gift in, then dashed to the porch, rang the bell and sprinted away. As soon as he was next to Eli, she gunned the engine and took off with all the speed of their other getaways, but this time there was no laughter.

He saw her glance in the rearview mirror, and turned to see for himself that Ariel was at the front door.

"Merry Christmas," Eli whispered.

Zac kept glancing at her as she drove them along Whedon's main street and he saw in Eli what he'd always seen...a beautiful heart. He knew she'd try to downplay it, but Eli Cartwright gave herself unstintingly to her students. She was generous with her ex. And Zac knew if she ever loved him, he'd be the luckiest man in the world.

And he also had no doubt there was no *if* left for him. He loved her.

Zac Keller loved Elinore Cartwright. And nothing would ever change that.

DEBORAH KELLER HAD A penchant for gathering people to her—especially, it appeared, during the holidays. Eli was just like the rest, happy to oblige her.

It was Christmas evening, and the Keller's family room was filled with family and friends...and people they barely knew.

Ariel and her aunt were sitting as close to the fringe as the ample room would allow. Deirdre Mayor wasn't what Eli had imagined. She didn't look as if she could be more than a few years older than Ariel, her niece.

Deirdre hadn't said much to anyone, and when Eli tried to engage her, asking about her job as a flight attendant, Deirdre had seemed so uncomfortable that Eli had finally abandoned the effort.

Eli had talked to her mom and dad that morning. Her mother spent most of the conversation apologizing for not being there for Christmas. "If we'd known you were pregnant we'd never have booked the cruise…." she said over and over.

Eli reassured them both that she'd be spending the day with the Kellers, and they'd all celebrate together next year with the baby, which was always a topic that was sure to brighten her mother's mood.

"Any idea what this is all about?" she whispered to Zac, who shook his head. After they'd had their dinner and cleaned up, they'd all been summoned to the family room.

Mrs. Keller stood up. "First, I want to say I'm so glad to have all my children with me, and our new friends as well. I'm hoping those new friends will indulge me as I read a letter I received several days ago."

From her pocket Mrs. Keller produced a couple sheets of paper. " 'Dear Mrs. Keller,'" she read, " 'Enclosed please find a copy of an essay Cecily wrote for my English class. The topic was, what does family mean to you.'

" 'My students frequently inspire me, but I don't think I've ever been brought to tears by an essay before. I believe this is something you and your entire family will treasure. Sincerely, Helen Asti.'"

Mrs. Keller shuffled her papers and took a deep breath, as if she were going to start reading some more, but Cessy interrupted. "Mom, please don't." Cessy hid her face in the arm of the couch. "I'm so embarrassed," she moaned with the drama that only a teen could muster.

"Cecily Keller, this is beautiful, and not only am I going to read it, I'm thinking about having it framed."

Cessy groaned even louder, and her sister Layla patted her shoulder.

"There's no stopping Mom when she gets like this," Dom said from his seat across the room.

"You're right, Dom, there's not." Mrs.

Keller cleared her throat. " 'My family, by Cecily Keller.'

" 'When I was in fourth grade, our class made cards for our families for Thanksgiving. We traced our hands and turned them into construction paper turkeys. After school, I ran out and gave mine to my mom when Leslie, a girl in my class, came up and said, 'You're supposed to give it to your mom.' I was confused and told her this was my mom, and she said it couldn't be 'cause we didn't match. Until that moment, I don't think I ever thought that way about my family.'

" 'Oh, I knew my brother Zac always called me cocoa because my skin is the color of chocolate, and there was no way to miss that Mom is as pale as a white person can get. But I never saw those differences.'

" 'After that, I did. I noticed the looks my family got when we went out together. None of us are alike. We have brown hair, black, reddish-brown and blond. Some of us are very tall, a few are vertically challenged.'

" 'When I was ten, we all went to Disney World and Mom made us wear matching T-shirts that proudly proclaimed The Kellers. We got looks there, too.'

" 'The fact that we all were so very different made us stand out, and any school kid will tell you that standing out can be a problem. So I hoped no one would notice.'

" 'The Kellers took me home weeks after I was born. I have biological parents, but I never knew them. Then when I was five, my biological father took me back. I still remember that day. My whole family stood on the porch as the social worker led me away to her car. I didn't understand what was going on. My mom had told me that I was going to live with my real dad, but I felt that my *real* father was the man on the porch physically holding my brother Zac, who was struggling to get to me. I was only five and I knew who my family was. The stranger the state decided should have custody was nothing to me. The six months he kept me were bad. I don't talk about them. But they taught me something.'

" 'Before, I wanted to hide how different my family was, but then I figured out that biology might determine your skin and hair color, it might determine if you're tall or short, but it's your family that makes up your heart. It's your family that makes you whole, the person you really are.'

" 'I took my family to school later that year

for show-and-tell. Though in fourth grade we'd really outgrown the tradition, Mom stood by me and my entire family showed up and let me introduce them to my class. And I told all those kids that my family didn't match on the outside, that we never would, but we matched on the inside and that's all that counts.'

" 'And that's what family means to me.'"

Eli was crying like everyone else was. The men were more circumspect about it, blinking rapidly, discreetly wiping their eyes, but they were crying, too.

"Mom," Cessy whined, "I can't believe you did that."

"And I can't believe my daughter wrote such a beautiful essay. I remember the day you took us to school, but you never said why you did it." Mrs. Keller brushed away her own tears. "Well, I'm going to frame this essay, Cessy, and some day when you're grown and have a family of your own, I'll show it to them, and let them know that matching on the outside doesn't matter to me…"

Zac leaned closer to Eli, whispering, "And it doesn't matter to me."

Gently, he put his hand on her stomach,

and Eli knew Zac Keller had accepted her baby, even if it wasn't his.

She took Zac's hand and squeezed it, letting him know she understood.

When their eyes met, she truly got what Cessy had teased them about—talking without saying a word. And she'd been right because Eli could see not only his feelings for her, but also for the baby.

Ariel and her aunt made their excuses a few minutes later. Ariel hadn't said more than an obligatory greeting to Eli, but she'd noticed the girl was wearing the necklace she'd had Zac tuck in the Christmas box. *Believe,* it proclaimed. And Eli silently wished that Ariel would learn to believe in herself, and to believe that things would work out. Until Ariel could do that, Eli would just believe for her.

She and Zac spent another couple hours at his parents'. It was loud, and a bit crazy, but Eli had to admit, she loved Zac's entire family.

He drove her home, and as they pulled into her drive, she asked, "Can you come in for a few minutes? I have something for you."

"That's funny because I have something

for you." Zac reached in the back and pulled out a bag, then followed Eli to the porch, where she dug through her purse for her keys.

"I don't always have this much trouble finding my keys. Maybe it happens when you're around because you make me nervous."

"Do I?" He'd moved closer and she could feel his warm breath on her very cold neck. But her shivers had nothing to do with the warmth, and everything to do with the proximity of him.

He affected her like no one ever had.

Finally, she snagged her keys and opened the door.

He made himself at home, taking off his coat and boots before she'd managed, and by the time she walked into the living room, he'd snapped on the lights and even plugged in her tree.

"While you're over there, grab the present wrapped in red."

He came back carrying it, with his shopping bag as well.

"You first, please," she said. "I've wanted to give it to you for more than a week."

He tore into the paper with childlike abandon. "Wow."

That was exactly the reaction she'd hoped for. "I'll confess, I asked your mom to find the pictures for me."

He held the painting gently studying it.

"I have a student who's so talented, and she really could use the extra money. It's not professional, but I think it's beautiful. Your mom said she's jealous because she said she's never managed to get everyone home at the same time for a family portrait and she's going to have Katie paint a second one for her."

The painting was of the Keller family. All six kids and Mr. and Mrs. Keller. After listening to Cessy's essay tonight, Eli was even more pleased with the picture.

"Eli, this is one of the best presents I've ever received." He leaned over and hugged her. "Seriously, the best." Zac reached down, grabbed his bag and thrust it at her. "Here. Open the smaller one first."

She was much neater at taking off the paper, mainly because she'd always loved dragging the suspense out. Right now, the box was potentially anything, but in a moment, she'd know what it was and the magic would be over.

So she slowly worked the bow off, then the

tape, and finally found a small tan, cardboard box and slid the lid off…and started laughing. While the box was small, it was rather large for a key ring. And as she held the silver key ring that looked as if someone had bedazzled it with the most gaudy jewels they could find, she continued laughing.

"When I saw it, it practically glowed, and I thought you might have an easier time finding something that shiny in your purse."

"Oh, I guarantee I will."

"Now, open the flat one." She did, and found tickets. "I got us season's tickets to the Broadway series at the Warner Theater. I couldn't help but notice that most of your CDs are show tunes."

For five years, Eli had done the philharmonic with Arthur. And she loved the music, but he'd never once asked, or noticed, that she loved Broadway even more. And here was Zac, who'd not only noticed, but had also bought tickets for them both.

The fact that their tickets added another layer of permanence should have felt rushed, but instead felt comforting. She liked the idea of Zac being around for a long time.

"I don't know much about Broadway," he continued, "but you'll teach me."

She'd barely managed a thank-you when he said, "Okay, the last one's not technically for you."

Eli took the much larger box from the bag and opened it. There was a chipped and well-used piggy bank.

"I know it's not the prettiest thing in the world, but it's all I had when I came to the Kellers'. I'd been in foster care for two years, and they moved me from home to home, and I brought that bank with me. I squirreled away every penny I found, and in my mind, I was going to save enough to run away."

Eli had a mental image of Zac as a little boy, clutching his piggy bank and dreaming his dreams. She blinked hard, fighting back the tears. Trying to lighten the mood, she gave it a small shake. "It's empty, now. So what did you do with your riches?"

"Yes, it's empty. After I'd been with Mom and Dad for about a year, the adoption was official and I finally figured out they weren't going to send me anywhere else. Then the Kellers asked me if I would mind having a little brother or sister. I told them, wait a minute and went upstairs and I emptied the bank. I took my fortune—all eight dollars and sixty-two cents—down to Mom. I didn't know how it worked, and guessed they were going to buy a brother or sister for me, and I wanted to help. It's been empty ever since and collecting dust at my place. For years it was my security blanket of sorts… The only thing that stayed the same. It occurred to me that maybe the baby could use a little security."

Eli ran her fingers lightly along the beat-up pig, then gently set it on the coffee table, and turned to kiss the amazing man who'd come into her life at the most unexpected time, her baby sandwiched between them.

CHAPTER NINE

> "When the mother first feels the baby move, it's just the slightest flutter. First-time moms might not recognize it for what it is. Soon, the baby's movements will be unmistakable."
>
> —*Pregnancy, Childbirth and Parenting for Teens,* by Mary Jeanne Lorei

"HAPPY VALENTINE'S, MOM," Eli said as she answered the phone on Sunday morning.

"How did you know it was me?"

Her mom had asked this question before, but anything more complicated than an electric mixer was out of her mother's comfort zone. "Caller ID, remember?"

"I forgot you were my little techno-geek." Her mother paused and asked, "I got that right, right? Techno-geek?"

Eli laughed. "Yes, you did." She took the phone with her into the laundry room.

"See, I do pay attention sometimes. And happy Valentine's Day to you, too. Are you doing anything special tonight?"

"Zac's taking me to lunch, then he's coming with me to my first childbirth class."

"Are you sure that's a good idea? Maybe Tucker could be your partner, or I could come home—"

Eli stopped. "Mom, we've been through this. Don't cut short your winter in Florida. You'll be home long before the baby's born. And come on, you've met Tucker. I'm sure she would come to the classes with me if I asked, but Mom, it's Tucker."

Eli pulled a towel from the dryer.

"Tucker has had a baby, so I'm sure she could handle it," her mother insisted.

"Handle it? Yes. But be a comforting support system? She was an Amazon when she gave birth. I think she grunted a couple times, but she was so stoic, even the nurses commented. I'd feel as if I had to live up to that, and Mom, I'm no Amazon."

Eli was realistic. She was going to try to do a natural childbirth, but if the pain got too intense, she reserved her right to have drugs. To be honest, she would have felt she was letting her friend down.

Plus, she wouldn't admit it to her mom, but she wanted Zac with her. They'd grown so much closer since Christmas and—

"Fine. I just worry about you and Zac."

"You like him." Her inflection made it sound like a statement, but it was a question.

"We liked him when we met him, Eli, but…"

The word hung there ominously. "But?"

"But your father and I worry. Things are going very fast between the two of you, and with all the changes in your life…" Her mother paused. "I want you to be careful. You've never been a fan of change. Do you remember when you were four and I made you give up your crib finally? It was three weeks until I slept again."

"Mom, I've heard the story but I don't remember."

"Or, how about when we moved to Whedon. You swore you would ride your bike every day to our old place. When you realized it was too far, you spent a day sitting in the principal's office because I could make you go to school, but I couldn't make you pay attention in class."

"Seven, Mom. I was in second grade." Eli did remember the move. It was traumatic for her. She'd missed the security of her old school and her established friends. She missed knowing where everything was in her house and room. All these years later, she remembered the feeling of a hole in her life.

"And you carried your blanket to school every day that whole year, stuffed in your bookbag so your new friends wouldn't know, but you just needed it near. I want to be sure that Zac isn't another blanket, something to keep near when you're going through a big change."

Eli felt a niggle of concern, but quickly pushed it aside. Zac wasn't merely convenient to have around. "He makes me happy, Mom. Happy in a way I can't remember being."

"I'm glad," her mom assured her.

"I know you worry, Mom. But this is one time you don't have to. Zac's good for me."

"I'll call tomorrow to see how your class goes tonight."

"Talk to you then."

Eli sat on the floor of her small laundry room, dirty clothes surrounding her. That worry niggled at her some more.

Was she just using Zac?

ZAC WASN'T SURE WHAT he'd expected at a childbirth class, but the instructor had started them off slowly. No birth video to feel squeamish about.

That was next week.

"Arthur came by yesterday." Eli collected her mat and coat, and was heading for the exit.

"Oh?"

"He's been talking to a psychologist who told him he should embrace and explore his feelings for the baby. So, he wants to try. I suggested that he could come with me to my next sonogram. Maybe seeing the baby live on the screen, moving and so very real would help him figure things out. He said he'd try to make it."

They stood in silence. While Zac understood her insistence that Arthur had a right to be involved with the baby, he was still hurt. He was supposed to go to that appointment with Eli and she'd just dumped him to make Arthur feel better.

Granted it was just one appointment, but what if somewhere down the line it was something else, something bigger?

"Zac, I'm sorry Arthur's changed our plans."

Zac wanted to tell her it was okay, that he understood. And he did understand, but he wasn't okay with it. And admitting that made him feel small.

He tried to think of some excuse, but his silence must have stretched too long because Eli spoke up.

"Is something wrong? Arthur's visit?" she asked.

"It's not really—" He stopped. "I could lie to you, but I won't. Yes, it's Arthur's visit. It's his ability to walk in and out of your life at will. The baby's his. He doesn't want it. He changes his mind by the minute. Well, I don't. I want you. I want you more than you can know. There's no waffling, no indecision."

"He's the baby's father." She waited for him to respond. When he didn't, she continued, "I told you this was a mistake, but you're the one who insisted that single moms date and that it shouldn't be any different for them." She turned as if to leave.

"Eli, I meant every word I said—"

She wheeled around and faced him, her cheeks flushed. "Then I don't understand. I'm not getting back with Arthur. I've made that clear. But he deserves to be a part of the baby's—his baby's—life if he wants to be."

"Eli, I care about you. Hell, that doesn't

even come close to covering how I feel about you...." Wasn't this the time to tell her that he loved her?

"But?" she prompted.

"Not *but,* an *and.* And I care about this baby."

"I still don't understand." She leaned against the doorjamb, both hands resting on her rounded stomach.

"Every time Arthur shows up, this feeling—" Zac shook his head. "I don't know how to explain it. It's not jealousy..."

"I'm glad because I've told you, I don't have feelings for Arthur anymore. He was familiar. Like teacher's in-service days the first Wednesday of every month, or grocery shopping on Saturdays. I'm not proud of the fact that I was willing to settle, but I don't feel anything else for Arthur."

"And yet, he's here. Waffling about whether he wants to be a part of the baby's life."

"He's the biological father, he has rights and— Damn it, Zac, we're going in circles here."

"I know we are. And if you were the kind of person who could ignore his rights, you wouldn't be the woman I've fallen—" He quickly switched direction. "Did I ever tell you about Cessy?"

It was a rhetorical question because Zac never talked about that time.

Eli shook her head. "No."

"She mentioned it in that essay at Christmas. I was in my twenties when Mom and Dad brought the tiniest baby I'd ever seen home. Mom laughed and said she might already have five kids, but she was a novice at the baby stuff. Diapers. Bottles. She'd never dealt with any of that before. Neither had any of us, but we were all older and pitched in and learned. Cessy didn't just have two parents doting on her, she had five siblings as well. We spoiled her."

"I wouldn't say spoiled. She's a beautiful girl inside and out."

Zac nodded. "I'd graduated college and was working alongside Dad at the store when Cessy… She was five and we were the only family she'd ever known, Eli. I was her big brother. She ran to me with boo-boos and secrets. Everything."

"So what happened?" Eli asked.

"Mom and Dad had been through adoption with the rest of us, but it was different with Cessy. There were more legal steps, and they—we all—were waiting for everything to clear so her adoption could be finalized. Her mother's rights were terminated at birth but there were problems with finding her biological father. When they did, he claimed he didn't know about her and that he wanted her."

Zac remembered his mother calling him, so hysterical that he couldn't understand a word she was saying. He'd driven to the house and found everyone in tears. "I wanted to fight. I'd have spent every cent I had and bankrupted the store if I had to in order to keep her. But Mom and Dad—Eli, they said Cessy's father had rights. I was furious that they didn't do something to stop it. They were her parents. We were her siblings. *We* were her family. No DNA test would change that."

"Oh, Zac—"

"The night before the social worker was to come for her, I gave her a necklace. A small gold circle. And I told her that it was a hug. That anytime she missed us she could press it close and it would be as if we were hugging her. She didn't understand then, but the next day…"

Ten years later, that morning was still

vivid in his memory. "She cried and screamed, Eli. Over and over."

TEARS WERE STREAMING DOWN Eli's face as she listened to Zac. She didn't even bother trying to wipe them away. Her heart was breaking for him, for Cessy, for the entire Keller family.

"I couldn't stop them," he continued, his voice ragged. "I couldn't save Cecily. I didn't lie, Eli. I can love your baby, sight unseen. It's not a question of that, it's a question of how will I survive if Arthur at some point takes…"

"Zac, it's not like that…Arthur's not taking anyone," she assured him.

"Eli, it is *just* like that. I want to be this baby's father."

Eli knew it was too soon to be talking in those terms, although she did wish Zac were the baby's father, too. "Listen, we're just dating—"

"There's more to us than just dating and you know that." She thought he was done, and maybe he'd thought so as well because he looked startled as he blurted out, "I love you. I love this baby. Maybe it's right to let Arthur in if he wants, but I don't give a damn, anymore than I cared when Cessy's father wanted her back."

"Zac, you're not being fair."

"I know that, damn it. I'm jealous of something that hasn't even happened. I'm scared of losing you and the baby."

"Zac…" She wanted to reach him, to tell him it would be all right, but she couldn't do that. Maybe it wouldn't.

She hugged the baby.

Zac took a step forward and held the door open for her. "It's my problem. I'll drop you off, then. I need to go and think."

"Zac, I never wanted to hurt you."

"I don't want to hurt you, either, and I know that I am, but I'm not sure what else to do."

"I should never have said yes to dating you. I knew it was—"

He silenced her with a kiss.

"I'm an ass. Confused about a lot of things, but I know one thing. The day you agreed to date me was one of the best days of my life. Please don't give up on me."

When they reached Eli's place, he gave her a peck on the cheek and said, "I'll call you tomorrow."

She headed toward her house, hoping he'd follow, hoping he'd come inside with her.

But Zac was gone.

So many things had changed in her life over the last six months. She'd handled all of them. Though, if she lost Zac…that might be the one thing she wouldn't recover from.

She thought about calling Tucker. Or her mom. But Tucker would just be furious with Zac for her sake, and she didn't want that. And her mom would be on the next plane home, and she didn't want that, either.

So, Eli didn't call anyone. She turned away from her front door and went for a stroll. The sidewalks were finally clear again, rather than snow-covered, although there was still plenty of snow in front yards and occasionally, where the day's melting snow had pooled, there was ice.

The moon was full and bright enough to create shadows on the snow of the bare trees.

She made it onto Main Street, where the stores were closed and dark. A few bars and a coffeehouse still had lights on, but it was a Thursday, so they weren't heavily populated, either.

She could already feel Zac's absence. How had he become such an important part of her life? They'd worked together for a while on the CATA Project, but over the last months they'd gotten so close.

He'd said he loved her.

The weight of those words hung heavily. He loved her, and she'd hurt him.

"Ms. Cartwright?"

She spotted Ariel waddling out of the coffeehouse toward her, slinging her coat on as she walked.

"Ms. Cartwright, are you okay?"

Ariel had been avoiding her ever since she told the class she was pregnant. Oh, she came to school and still went to her job at Keller's Market, but the connection Eli had felt with her was broken. "Sure, I'm fine. Why wouldn't I be fine?"

They stood under a streetlight, which illuminated the fact that Ariel's stomach was swollen to the extent that she couldn't zip up her coat. Eli worried about her out in the cold. "You'd better get inside."

"Come with me. I'll treat you to a decaf coffee or tea."

"No, that's fine—"

"Ms. Cartwright, I know I've been a jerk. I've known all along I was being a jerk, but I didn't know how to stop. It seems once you start, it can grow exponentially, picking up steam on its own."

"You weren't a jerk. I let you down." And

now, she'd let Zac down as well. If she could handle Arthur a different way she would, but she couldn't.

"No. I just finally figured out you were human." Ariel offered Eli a wry smile that was so much older than her seventeen years. "I'm sorry."

"It's okay, Ariel. I understand…understood."

"Well, show me that you really forgive me. Let me buy you an herbal tea."

Eli didn't know how to say no after that, so she followed Ariel to the coffeehouse. After the dark sky, the well-lit room seemed overly bright.

She and Ariel sat down at a table. "Ms. Cartwright, you're not okay."

Eli could see the concern on the girl's face. "Yes, yes, I'm fine. How about you? How are things at your aunt's?"

"The same. She said I could quit work if I wanted, but I like it at the grocery store. Everyone's been nice. They had a shower for me last week, did I tell you?"

Eli didn't point out that Ariel hadn't been saying much of anything to her outside of the classroom, but she didn't mention it. "No."

"It was great. I got all kinds of stuff for the baby. Mr. Keller even got me a crib."

Zac hadn't mentioned it, but then he wouldn't. He wasn't the type of man who did things in order to be praised. He did them because they needed to be done. "He's a very nice man."

"And a good boss."

Eli nodded. "I'm so glad the store's working out for you. I have two other businesses in town lined up for CATA." She needed to get that organized before she had the baby. There was so much to do before the baby came.

Where would Arthur or Zac be when that happened? When she first found out about the baby, she'd thought Arthur would stand by her, but it soon became apparent that wasn't going to happen. Then for months, she'd believed Zac would be there.

And now, maybe he wouldn't.

If he walked, she wouldn't blame him. When he'd told her about Cessy, she realized that it wasn't a story he shared with people, and she'd also realized how the idea of Arthur popping in and out of the baby's life must hurt and scare him.

And while she understood, she couldn't help but feel as if her heart was breaking.

Eli started to cry. Not a few dainty tears. But rather big wet drops that ran down her cheeks. Her nose immediately clogged and she took a napkin and wiped it.

"Ms. Cartwright, it's okay. Being pregnant makes you cry and stuff. But this isn't about being pregnant, is it?"

"I think I just lost…" She couldn't even say his name. "I mean, having the baby's father leave me hurt, but to lose…" It occurred to her that she was about to unburden herself to an already overburdened student. "Never mind. You're right. It's only hormones."

"I'll go get you that tea," Ariel offered.

While she was gone, Eli took a tissue from her pocket and tried to get herself under control as she sipped her tea and listened to Ariel's chatter. The girl was keeping up a running commentary for her sake, trying to distract her.

It was sweet.

It wasn't working, but it was really sweet.

"So, how are the childbirth classes coming?" Eli asked.

"My aunt went with me. Hee hee hoo. Hee hee hoo," she breathed. "I'm pretty good. She tries to help, but ends up out of breath in the end." Ariel paused and asked, "Are you taking classes?"

"Sure." She'd taken them with Zac. Maybe she should ask Tucker to take over for him.

"I wasn't sure." Ariel dumped another bag of sugar into her teacup. " I mean, you're a teacher and have taught this stuff for so many years."

"Ariel, I may have taught it, but I never lived it. I think you and I are both going to find out that the reality of it is so much different than just reading about it."

"Oh, I've already discovered that. I'd read about morning sickness, but you don't get how bad it can be until you spend every morning and most evenings kneeling in front of a toilet, hoping you can keep something down." She nodded. "So, who's your partner?" she asked.

"A friend."

"Someone I know?"

Eli didn't want to answer. Ariel was finally talking to her again, and she didn't want to blow that.

"I'm teasing, Ms. Cartwright. I know you and Mr. Keller are dating, that he's going with you."

"Ariel, Mr. Keller and I—"

"Ms. Cartwright, I meant it. I know I was a jerk. I know your baby's dad left, and that Mr. Keller likes you."

"How?" Eli asked.

"He came to see me right after you told us you were pregnant. He basically told me I was acting like a spoiled brat and to get over it."

"He shouldn't have spoken to you like that…at all."

"He didn't put it that way. He was a lot more polite about it, but I could see how much he cared about you. And even after I didn't follow his advice, he's still been really nice to me at work. He's the best boss I ever had. One of the nicest guys I've ever met. If I were a little older…" Her grin said quite clearly she was joking.

Eli laughed.

"Here's the thing, Ms. Cartwright. It's easy to get wrapped up in yourself when you're pregnant. They don't say it in the books, but it's probably part of the whole process. I mean, every day your body changes, the baby grows. You have to worry about what you eat and pretty much anything you do may be affecting the baby. So, it makes sense that everyone who's pregnant spends so much time thinking about themselves. It's not a bad thing. It just is. That's what happened with me. I forgot that you're human. And that's why I was mad. It was all about me. But maybe you've got some of that, too, and you don't see how lucky you are having Mr. Keller around. I know the baby's father was a skunk—"

"He's not. It's just that this baby wasn't what he had planned." Eli defended Arthur out of habit more than a firm belief that he wasn't a skunk.

"Yeah? Too freakin' bad for him. Charlie said the same thing when he walked—that he didn't sign up for a baby. Really? Well, I didn't either, and neither did you. And yet, here we are, two very knocked-up women handling it. They're both rat bastards, if you ask me. But Mr. Keller, he didn't walk away. He stayed. And it's not even his baby. That makes you lucky in my book."

Ariel got quiet and turned to look out the window, giving Eli a moment to process what her student had just said.

She was lucky.

Zac didn't like Arthur walking in and out? That was understandable.

He'd admitted it to her and shared a traumatic event from his past in order to make her understand. That was honest and brave.

He'd said he loved her and that he loved her baby sight unseen.

Coming from some men, that might be a line, but with Zac, she knew there was honesty in the statement.

She hadn't been nearly as honest with him. She owed him that.

"Ariel, I need to go, but I want to thank you. You've helped me work through some things. And I really… well, thank you."

"You know how you said that being pregnant is different than teaching it?"

Eli nodded.

"Well, looking at other people's lives and giving advice is easier than figuring your own out."

"You are a very wise girl…." She paused and corrected herself. "Woman. You're a very wise woman, Ariel Mayor. And I know you're going to make something out of yourself. That you've got a wonderful life in front of you…you and this baby."

Ariel reached out and took her hand. "You, too, Ms. Cartwright."

"Thank you. And right now, there's a person I really need to talk to because of you."

Eli hurried home, got her car and drove to Zac's. She didn't want to take time to think anything through. She just wanted to get to him and say the words that were suddenly burning to come out.

She knocked on his door and he answered, looking horrible.

"I know you want to be alone and think, but I wanted to tell you that I think I love you, too. I don't want to pressure you. I understand your feelings about Arthur. And if he wants to see this baby, to be a part of its life, I'll let him. But there's no chance of him being a part of mine again, at least not romantically. Days, weeks, months have gone by, and I don't miss him. But one evening of you leaving early and I feel bereft. I missed you."

"Say it again."

She stood on her tiptoes and kissed his cheek. "I love you. I just wanted you to know. I owed you the same honesty that you'd given me."

Eli turned and started to walk away, but Zac grabbed her hand and gently pulled her into his arms, and kissed her. His feelings right there on the surface. He loved her. He loved her baby. He wanted her.

He held her as if she were in fact the most beautiful woman in the world.

All her worries and doubts fell away.

He led her into the house and kicked the door shut. There was an urgency in his kiss, but despite that there was tenderness in it, too. She still had her coat on as she stood sandwiched between him and the wall, locked in a kiss that she hoped would never end.

And when it did, when he finally withdrew, there was an almost physical ache.

"Say it again." Zac looked at her, his need evident in his expression.

"I love you," she said for a third time, the words coming out so much easier this time. "I love you. It's a crazy time to fall in love, but I don't think love follows a schedule. I can't pinpoint the moment it happened. It sort of crept up on me so slowly I didn't even realize it. Somewhere between that lunch last fall, when I told you Arthur and I had broken up, and today, I fell in love with you. And I know you have concerns. So do I, but—"

"Not now. Not tonight. Any concerns or problems will be there tomorrow."

And he kissed her again.

Part of Eli knew she should protest. She

wasn't the type to bury her head in the sand and ignore issues. She liked to face them head-on. But as Zac deepened the kiss, the only thing she could think of was getting even closer.

He held her with one arm, but his free hand moved down and rested lightly between them on her belly.

Eli didn't think she was self-conscious, but she felt shy about her ever-changing body.

"Zac, I—"

"Shh. You're beautiful, Eli. The most beautiful woman I've ever seen." He stroked her stomach. "And this baby. I meant it when I said, I've fallen in love with it, too." He gently caressed her stomach. "I want to be here for you now, and after it's born. I'm in this, Eli. No matter what, I'm in this."

He didn't mention Arthur, but she knew that her ex still troubled Zac.

"But—"

"No. Not tonight. We'll work it all out. Right now, I want you to stay with me. Spend the night."

It was what she wanted, too.

But she must have hesitated too long because Zac added, "I mean, I could just hold you, if doing more would hurt the baby."

He was giving her an out. She could spend the night in Zac's arms without making love to him. And yet, despite the fact she felt ungainly and shy, somehow, because it was Zac, it didn't matter. "There's no problem."

That was the only invitation he needed. He took her hand and led her to his room.

"I'm nervous," she confessed as she looked at his bed. It was a bachelor's room. Spartan in its furnishing. A bed, sheets and blankets, a nightstand with a stack of books and a chest of drawers.

"Eli, seriously, just spend the night with me. We'll sleep. I want to hold you. I could hold you forever and it wouldn't be enough."

And as she looked at him, Eli knew he meant it, which eased her shyness. She walked back into his arms and kissed him, then reached up to unbutton his dress shirt.

He pulled back. "Are you sure?"

She nodded.

Carefully, he tugged her shirt up over her head. Her breasts were huge. Well, not huge, but significantly larger than they'd ever been. Even in her no-nonsense maternity bra, she felt exposed.

And when she glanced down, she realized she'd worn her maternity pants that had the elastic panels in the sides. They looked like normal pants, although her stomach seemed huge to her as she peered down at it.

Zac's shirt was unbuttoned and he tore that off as well, and quickly slipped out of his white, cotton T-shirt.

She thought he'd remove more clothing, but as if sensing her feelings, he didn't. Instead, he took her hand and led her to the bed.

"You look beautiful."

He gently placed a hand on her stomach. At that moment, the baby kicked.

"That's amazing."

"It doesn't freak you out?"

"I love you," he said. "I love this baby. Nothing about being with you freaks me out."

And she saw in his eyes that he meant every word. He didn't see her ponderously large breasts or swollen abdomen. He saw her. Just her. And he thought she was beautiful.

And because he did, she felt truly beautiful. There was no more awkwardness, no more hesitancy. She gave him everything she had.

He was gentle and tender as they learned each other's bodies.

She forgot to be self-conscious. She forgot everything but this man…this moment.

In his arms she felt safe.

She felt treasured.

She felt loved.

And for tonight, that was enough.

CHAPTER TEN

"The third trimester is a time of change. Your pregnancy is even evident to strangers. You're gaining weight and your body is changing almost daily. Most women find this troubling, possibly scary. Just remind yourself that these are normal reactions for both teens, and for older moms. And that we must embrace our fear and not let it beat us down."

—*Pregnancy, Childbirth and Parenting for Teens,* by Mary Jeanne Lorei

A MONTH AND A HALF.

Zac couldn't help but marvel at how happy he'd been the last six weeks. Cessy complained last week that if he didn't stop his incessant smiling his face was going to get stuck like that.

As he watched Eli, he knew he was

grinning in a way Cessy would have commented on if she were here. Eli was slicing apples for a pie, one fell and landed on her protruding stomach.

He chuckled.

"Hey, men who laugh at pregnant ladies using their stomachs as a shelf don't get apple pie."

"Oh, I'll mind my manners, then."

"Good." She went back to slicing, looking as happy as he felt.

Tucker announced her presence by coughing loudly. "Okay, you two—" she paused. "Don't get all lovey-dovey."

Tucker was wearing paint-splattered clothes. She'd sided with him when he insisted that Eli not be in the baby's room while it was being painted, even though they'd used a low VOC paint.

Tucker had finished the edging so he could grab a bite to eat before he left for the office.

Zac listened to the two of them banter. They might not be related, but there was a sisterly connection. He had a vast degree of experience in how sisters sounded.

"Eli, I'm going to run home, shower and head to the market. But I'll be back before dinner."

"Don't be late, or I call the pie," Tucker said.

"A piece of the pie?" Eli asked.

Tucker shook her head. "Nope, I meant the whole pie."

"I'll definitely be back in time," Zac promised as he leaned over and kissed Eli goodbye.

"Okay, come on, you two. As Bart would say, no sucking face in front of me."

"You realize that if Bart was saying that to you, you must have been kissing someone," Zac teased.

"Not me. He said it about my pop. Turns out my father's got a new girlfriend and Bart walked in on them saying goodbye. I was sympathetic when he told me, but the two of you have made me even more so."

Zac laughed.

"Keep Eli out of that room," he said as he walked toward the front door.

"I've been watching out for Eli for years."

Eli waved a hand at both of them. "Hey, you two, I'm here and I'm quite capable of watching out for myself."

"Right," Tucker scoffed.

"I know you are," Zac said as they walked to the front door. "But I worry."

"You don't have to worry, Zac. I'm a big

girl." She paused and added, "I'm older, remember? More years of experience."

That she was able to tease him about their age difference, which had once been a cause for concern with her, meant she was becoming more comfortable with the idea.

"I'll hurry," he promised as he kissed her again.

Kissing Eli.

Making love to Eli.

He put on his coat, leaned down for one more quick buss on the cheek, then opened the door to the raw wind.

A car pulled up in front of Eli's house and Arthur got out. It was as if the man had radar and could sense when Zac was happy.

"You're here again?" Arthur asked as he spotted him.

"I was just about to ask you the same question," Zac said.

At the last minute, Arthur had called off going with Eli to her sonogram appointment, and neither Zac, nor Eli had seen or heard from him since. Zac lived in hope that the man had finally given up.

Arthur didn't respond. He continued walking up to Eli's front door.

It took all of Zac's self-restraint not to

follow him. But Eli was right. She was a big girl and had been taking care of herself for years. She could handle Arthur.

Right?

"WELL, YOU TWO ARE GETTING all hot and heavy," Tucker said once Eli returned to the kitchen after seeing Zac off.

"Maybe." She could feel her cheeks burning as Tucker grinned in that knowing way of hers. "You know, your teasing us wasn't very helpful."

"Oh, come on. If you walked in on me sucking face, you'd be teasing me relentlessly."

Anxious to turn the conversation away from herself and Zac, Eli asked, "Speaking of which. Whatever happened to that guy who kept asking you out?"

"I kept saying no."

"And?"

Tucker shrugged. "I haven't seen him for a couple months. He told me he had business out of town and he'd call me when he came back. I told him not to bother."

Eli sat down on the stool next to her. "Oh, Tucker."

"You said 'oh, Tucker, but I heard 'poor Tucker' in your voice." Tucker stirred her cup of tea, concentrating on it rather than looking at Eli.

"He sounded nice," Eli prompted.

She worried about Tucker. Worried that one day she'd chase away the right man for her.

"Sure, nice if you like designer suits."

"And if he wore jeans? Would that have helped?"

"Maybe. But he doesn't. Zac does. He looked fairly perfect in his painting jeans today." Tucker blatantly changed the topic back to Eli. "But."

"But he's not perfect, either. I mean, if he were a few years older he would be—"

"The age difference doesn't seem to be stopping you," Tucker interrupted.

"—and if I weren't pregnant, maybe we'd be perfect. Or maybe not. Maybe perfection doesn't enter into love."

"Oh, are we tossing the L word around already?"

Eli was saved from having to answer by a knock at the kitchen door. She glanced out the window and sighed, opening it. "Arthur?"

"Talk about a lack of perfection," Tucker muttered, then took a sip of her tea.

Eli wasn't sure if Arthur was glaring at Tucker because he'd heard her comment, or if he was just glaring at Eli because it was Saturday. The two of them had never needed much of a reason to do some glaring.

"Arthur, what did you need?"

"I need to talk to you."

So much for him just handing her the papers nullifying his parental rights. "Fine."

He obviously detected her lack of enthusiasm and frowned. He nodded in Tucker's direction. "Somewhere she isn't."

Tucker didn't even bother looking up from her tea. "I know that was a hint, pal, but I'm not leaving you alone with Eli. If you want privacy, try the living room, but I'll be in the house."

"You think I'd hurt her?" Arthur sounded affronted to his very core.

"You proved you would when she told you about the baby, didn't you?" Tucker asked. "Or how about last month, when you stood her up at the—"

"Okay, you two, enough." Eli thought about asking Tucker to leave, but that particular stubborn gleam in her friend's eye told her there wasn't much hope of that, so she said, "Come into the living room, Arthur, and say what you need to say."

Eli thought about sitting and offering him

a seat, but she didn't want to drag this visit out longer than necessary, so she stood in the middle of the room.

"Now, what?" Her question came out sharper than she intended. "Sorry. What did you need, Arthur? Did you see the lawyer again?"

"Yes, I saw him."

"And the papers?"

"I have them, Eli, but I still haven't signed them yet."

"Arthur—"

"I can't, Eli. I've tried. I've tried over and over, but I can't. I miss you."

"Arthur…" She didn't know what else to say. She'd pretty much said it all again and again.

"How is the baby…?" He choked out the word *baby*.

"Everything's fine. The doctor's keeping a close eye on the two of us because of my age."

"If your age is an issue, then what about mine?" He tried to play it off as a joke, but it fell flat. "I mean, I'm a member of AARP. That's too old to be a first-time father."

Eli grabbed the notepad and pen out of the end table drawer and wrote. "Here's my doctor's name, the address and the appointment date and time. It's up to you." She didn't want to give him another chance. She remembered how Zac had reacted last time, and didn't want to start that up again.

She didn't have a choice, Arthur was the baby's father.

"I do miss you," Arthur said.

"Arthur, I'm sorry—"

"Yeah." He took the piece of paper from her outstretched hand. "I'll see you there."

He retraced his steps toward the kitchen.

Eli followed him. She felt bad for him, and yet, she could hardly remember the time when she thought she loved him.

He turned before he reached the kitchen. "Maybe just a dinner?"

She shook her head. "But I'll see you at the sonogram."

He nodded.

Tucker was washing dishes, and as soon as she spotted Arthur, she seemed ready to shoot out another zinger, but Eli shook her head, and Tucker's lips clamped shut. Arthur slipped his boots on and went out the door.

"So?" Tucker brought a mug of hot tea over and slid it in front of Eli.

"He's going to try another sonogram appointment. Maybe if he sees the baby, he'll feel more connected."

"Why? Why do you keep giving him chances? Just tell him to back off."

"He has rights, Tucker."

"You're a better woman than I am, Eli. If Bart's father came back today and wanted to explore his rights, I'd…well, let's just say, I wouldn't be inviting him to a sonogram appointment for a second time."

"I'm no better. And I'm ashamed to admit that there's a part of me that would like nothing more than to tell him to kiss off. But I've worked with girls in this situation for too many years. I've worked with some of the fathers, too. It's not an easy position for any of them. I always encourage my girls to give the baby's father a chance. How can *I* do any less? What kind of hypocrite would that make me?"

"I don't think I'd care. And that, my friend, is the difference between us and why you are indeed a better woman than I am. So, what do you want to do now? We could go see a movie or something. Bart's on a date—" Tucker stopped and looked as if she'd swallowed a bug. "I hate that my kid is old enough to date. Anyway, he's out. I'm footloose and fancy-free, so a movie, or—"

The phone rang and Eli held up a finger. "Hold on to that thought." She picked up the receiver in the living room. "Hello?"

"Eli, it's Zac. I was at the store and Ariel was working." He was all out of breath.

"Is something wrong?" A sense of panic filled Eli. Things between her and Ariel had finally become normal.

"I'm driving her to the hospital now. She's in labor. Her aunt's on a flight and is trying to get home, but she won't be back until later tonight, and her parents still aren't talking to her, so—"

"Which hospital?" Eli asked.

"St. Vincent's," Zac told her.

"Got it. I'm on my way."

"We're not that far ahead of you. I'd have just come to get you, but Ariel thought maybe her aunt would be home and able to come. So we stopped there, and I don't want to backtrack." He paused and added, "She shouldn't be alone."

"It's fine, Zac. I'll be there as soon as I can." She hung up and forced herself to take a deep breath. She talked about moments like this with her girls. It was easy to get frazzled and just run, but it was better to take a moment, a breath and just think.

What did she need? What might Ariel need?

"Eli?"

She'd forgotten all about Tucker.

"Sorry, the movie will have to wait. That was Zac. Ariel's in labor and her aunt's out of town, so he's driving her to the hospital in Erie."

"And you're going, too." There was no question, just a statement. "I'll drive you."

"I can drive myself," Eli insisted. "Besides, sitting around a waiting room would be less than exciting for you."

"I know, but hey, we'll have chick bonding all the way there and back again."

"Chick bonding?" Eli laughed because to the best of her knowledge, Tucker worked mainly with men, and seemed to prefer their company. "You hate chick bonding."

"Well, maybe most of the time, but not with you. There's a difference between spending time with women friends and spending it with guy friends. Women want to talk and be all feely about things. Guys just want you to pass the beer and pay attention to the game. They are simple creatures and easy to entertain."

Eli was grateful Tucker was giving her something to think about other than Ariel and she happily played along. "I thought this guy who wants to date you was giving you grief?"

"He's an anomaly. He's all touchy-feely. Mr. Designer Suit is part girl. Not in any physical way or in his mannerisms—no, he's all man there."

Tucker paused, and in any other woman, Eli would have been sure that the escaping hiss of air was a sigh of appreciation, but with Tucker she wasn't. It could just as easily have been exasperation.

"But emotionally? He's the girl." Tucker got a look in her eye that was definitely dreamy. And Eli was pretty sure the dreaminess had more to do with the all-man parts than the emotionally girly parts.

"Tuck, for someone who swears she's not interested, we do seem to talk about him a lot."

"Let's go," Tucker grumbled.

It wasn't a long ride from Whedon to Erie. It normally took Eli about twenty minutes on I-79. But with Tucker behind the wheel, they made it in fifteen. Still, it felt pretty close to forever to Eli. She was worried about Ariel.

Tucker parked her four-wheel-drive pickup in record time, too, and Eli hurried into the hospital. She checked in at the front desk, got Ariel's room number, then strode to the elevators. Tucker stuck close by until they passed by the waiting room. "This is where I stay."

"You don't have to. I—"

Tucker's stubborn expression, which Eli knew so well, was firmly set in place. "I'll wait, Eli. What else do I have to do other than sit around at home and wait for Bart? It annoys him when I wait up, so I'd rather wait here for you. And I'm going to confess, I really feel for the kid. I knew my dad would be pissed, but I never for a moment doubted he'd be there for me. Since her parents aren't here, I'll be."

Despite her cumbersome size, Eli hugged Tucker. As always, it seemed to catch her friend by surprise.

"Fine, Tuck. I'll come fill you in when I can."

She continued down the hall to find the birthing room, then softly knocked on the door. "Come in," Ariel called.

Ariel was in the bed with a very pale Zac standing by her side. "You're here." There was relief written all over his expression.

Eli went directly to Ariel's side. "I am," she said to Zac, then turned her attention to Ariel. "How are you doing, honey?"

"The doctor said I'm on the early side of things, but not to worry. Oh, and Mr. Keller is about to hyperventilate if he tries breathing with me one more time."

"Zac, Tucker's in the waiting room if you'd like to join her there."

Instead of the gratitude she expected, he put on a brave face. "I can stay if you want. Ariel was exaggerating. I'm a great breather."

Suddenly, Ariel started to take long, deep breaths.

"Oh, it's another one. I recognize the signs by now," Zac blurted. "I'll let you handle it and just wait with Tucker."

"SO MUCH FOR MALE BRAVADO," Zac heard Eli say as he beat a very hasty retreat.

Zac didn't care if running out of the birthing room was cowardly. He wasn't ready for this.

He all but sprinted the waiting room and found Tucker sitting there. She looked up and snorted. "Wimped out?"

"They didn't need me there. No teen mom

wants her boss around while she's in labor." The argument sounded plausible. Logical even.

"Wimped out, huh?" Tucker repeated.

Zac flopped onto the rather hard sofa and made an actual thwapping noise. "Yeah."

"Hey, you drove the kid to the hospital. I'd have called an ambulance for her." She gave a little shudder. "Laboring moms? Ick. The thought gives me the heebie-jeebies."

"You had a baby," Zac felt obliged to point out.

Tucker nodded her agreement. "Yeah, and since I've been there, done that, I can categorically say that I wouldn't recommend the experience to anyone. They talk about a rush of mother's love the second you hold your baby. My first thought was, 'ew, someone clean him off.' "

Zac laughed and felt more centered.

"But the love did kick in."

He'd seen Tucker with her son and he knew it hadn't just kicked in, it went into overdrive.

She quickly grew more serious. "Can I ask you something?"

"Sure," he said hesitantly. He was the first to admit as Eli's best friend, Tucker had the right to ask him questions, but that didn't mean he'd want to answer.

She didn't look any happier about asking them. "Since Eli's father is still in Florida, I'm going to fill in for him and ask, just what are your intentions toward Eli?"

"Pardon?" He wasn't sure what he thought she'd ask, but this wasn't it.

"I mean, you're there so often that you've become a fixture. You take her out on dates, but you also are just as comfortable hanging out with her. You're helping her get ready for a baby...for a baby that's not yours. I just want to know where you see this going."

"Where do I see it going? I see me and Eli, sitting in rockers on our front porch, grey-haired and wrinkled." As he said the words, he could indeed picture it. The two of them after a lifetime together. "Does that answer your question?"

Tucker shrugged. "Yes, I think it does. But does Eli know that's where you see this heading?" Before he could answer, she added, "When Arthur bailed, she recovered quickly. But since there's already more between the two of you than she ever had with him... I just don't want to see her hurt."

"I don't plan on hurting her."

"That I believe, but you have the power to. So be careful."

Zac didn't say anything after that, and neither did Tucker, for which he was grateful. He thought about her words. He had the power to hurt Eli.

What Tucker hadn't mentioned was that Eli had the power to hurt him.

HOURS LATER, ELI WASN'T sure just how many—the only time that mattered was the time between contractions, and that was growing shorter and shorter for Ariel—and there was still no baby.

"Come on, Ariel, you're doing great." Eli changed, "Hee hee hoo. Hee hee hoo. Long, slow breaths. You can do this."

The contraction ended and Ariel sank back against the pillow. "I don't want to do this, Ms. Cartwright. I want Charlie back. I want my mother here. I want my aunt. I don't want to do this."

Eli's heart broke for Ariel. She was a special girl who deserved to have her parents at her side. "Concentrate, sweetie."

"I called my mom. She just hung up on me."

Another contraction caught Ariel. Eli

could recognize the signs now. "Breathe," she commanded again.

They fell into a rhythm.

Contraction. Rest a moment.

Contraction. Rest.

The doctor came in. "Let's see how we're doing." She positioned Ariel's feet in the stirrups and preformed a quick examination. "Ariel, you're one hundred percent effaced. You can push whenever you feel the urge."

Two contractions later, Ariel started pushing. The next forty minutes were a blur. Eli might not have been the one giving birth, but when the doctor held a baby aloft and cried, "It's a girl," she felt as exhausted and elated as Ariel.

"You have a daughter, Ariel," she whispered as she brushed the girl's sweat-sopped hair off her forehead.

"A girl," Ariel murmured as the nurse covered the baby up and handed her to Ariel. "Isn't she the most beautiful thing ever, Ms. Cartwright?"

"She is, Ariel. She is."

Ariel held the baby close and without looking up from her daughter asked, "Do you think you'd call Charlie and tell him. I mean,

I'm not asking him to come over, or anything, but he should know he has a daughter."

"I'll go call him."

"And my mom? I mean, I know she hung up on me, but…"

But. Eli could read so much in that one word. But Ariel was hoping her mother would have a change of heart and come— that her mother loved her enough to be there now when she needed her.

"I'll call them both. I'll tell Tucker and Mr. Keller, too."

Ariel didn't look up from her daughter. "Do you think they want to meet her?"

"I think they'd love it, if you're up to it?"

"Just give us twenty minutes or so, okay?" the doctor asked. "We can have everyone cleaned up and comfortable by then."

"I'll be back in twenty," Eli promised, then she leaned down and did what Ariel's mom should have been there to do. She kissed Ariel's forehead. "Congratulations, hon. You did great."

She wanted to tell Ariel that as of this moment everything had changed. That being a mother was going to alter her views, but there was time enough for that later.

In the hallway, she telephoned Charlie

Markowski. She'd gotten all Ariel's contact numbers weeks earlier and was glad of it.

Eli had to leave a message on Charlie's voice mail, and that was fine with her because all Eli could think of was Ariel crying for her mother, her aunt…and for Charlie. She was afraid her feelings would shine through if they had a conversation. Voice mail was easier.

Next, she called Ariel's aunt, and again got voice mail. This time, she wished she'd actually spoken to Deirdre, who must still be in the air.

Finally, she called Ariel's mom.

"Mrs. Mayor, this is Ariel's teacher, Eli Cartwright. I'm at the hospital. She has a baby girl and—"

There was a click on the other end as Ariel's mother disconnected.

Eli had seen parents write off their daughters before, and she couldn't understand it. "No matter what happens to you, I'll always be here for you," she whispered to her baby, who was currently turning somersaults from the way it was kicking.

She hurried down the hall.

"It's a girl," she announced to Zac and Tucker in the waiting room.

"Come, sit down for a minute," Zac said. "This couch isn't exactly plush, but you look as if you need a break."

"That was the most amazing thing I've ever seen. Exhausting, but amazing. Let me tell you, I'm pretty sure that prepared me for childbirth better than any class film."

She sank back, closed her eyes and sighed.

ZAC SMILED AT TUCKER as they both realized that Eli wasn't merely resting her eyes, she was dozing.

He watched her as she slept. Her hands were folded on her stomach. He was startled when they moved, as if Eli had the hiccups. It took him a second to realize it was the baby.

The baby had hiccups.

It was a person in its own right. Soon, they'd be back at the hospital and Eli would be the one cradling her new baby.

Hers and Arthur's.

He frowned.

"What's that for?" Tucker asked.

He'd forgotten she was still there.

"Just thinking."

"Thinking not exactly good thoughts."

He shrugged. "When Eli has the baby, where will I fit in?"

"I'm guessing this is about Arthur," Tucker said with a frown that Zac wasn't sure he could read. Either she was frowning at the mention of Arthur's name, or she was frowning about his concerns about Eli's ex.

"Listen, Zac—"

Whatever Tucker wanted him to listen to would have to wait as the nurse came in and said, "Ariel and the baby are waiting for you all. Don't stay too long, okay? They both need some rest."

Eli jumped awake and rubbed her eyes, looking slightly disoriented.

"Ariel's ready," Zac repeated.

"Let's go." She led them down the hall, then turned and asked, "How long was I asleep?"

"Not long," Zac assured her.

"You snored," Tucker teased. "Loud."

Eli didn't look as if she really believed Tucker, but Zac could see the small thread of doubt. "Did I?"

"No," he answered. She looked relieved. He added, "Well, not that loud, anyway."

She looked chagrined, then caught his smile. "Nice, you guys. Just pick on the tired pregnant woman."

She stopped in front of Ariel's door and knocked softly.

"Come in."

They walked in and Ariel looked content, as she sat cradling her baby.

She beckoned them closer. "Isn't she perfect?"

It was no hardship to admit she was. Ariel's daughter had a thatch of blond hair that was so pale it was almost white. She had a round face and brilliant blue eyes.

"She's beautiful, Ariel," Zac said as Eli cooed over the baby.

Tucker made a noise of affirmation, and though she didn't coo, she appeared decidedly mushy as she looked at the baby.

Ariel held her out to Eli. "Would you like to hold her?"

Eli took the baby as Ariel said, "I'm going to name her Elinore Charlotte Mayor and call her Nora."

"Oh," Eli said, and started to cry. With a loud sniff, she spluttered, "Ariel, thank you, that's such an honor." And she pulled the blanket back and gently touched the baby's cheek.

Something in Zac melted at the sight of her cradling the newborn. The baby rested on her own baby bump.

Little Nora yawned, and Eli laughed.

"Look at her, Zac. Isn't she lovely? I can't believe that soon I'll be holding my baby."

Zac reached out and touched the baby's downy hair. "She's going to turn all the boys' heads in school, Ariel."

"And you know, as much as I chafed at my parents' restrictions, I can suddenly understand them better," Ariel admitted. There was a wistfulness in her voice, and Zac wished there was something he could do for her. He and Eli could support Ariel, but they weren't her parents. And he knew Ariel was hurt by their unwillingness to forgive her.

After cooing and cuddling the baby, Eli passed little Nora to Tucker, who despite her avowals in the waiting room, didn't show even the slightest baby bias.

"Zac?" Tucker held the baby toward him.

Not knowing what else to do, he took the baby. He'd never held one this small—Cessy had been a few weeks old when she'd come home, and a lot more filled out than Nora was. But as he peered down at her, he was amazed at how perfectly every feature was arranged. She yawned again, and opened her bright blue eyes and he would have testified in a court of law that she looked at him. Directly at him.

It was that easy—Zac felt connected to

this littlest bit of humanity. "Ariel, you take as long as you need off from work, and you let me know—me, not the store—if you need anything, because our little Nora will never want for anything. I promise you that."

He couldn't make up for the people who'd deserted her, but he could help wherever she needed him to.

He was still holding Nora and planning a trip to the store tomorrow to buy out the baby supplies section, when the door opened and a gangly boy walked in. "Ariel, I…"

The kid stopped as if he didn't know what else to say and even without an introduction, Zac knew this was Nora's father.

"Can I hold her?" the boy asked Ariel.

Zac looked to Ariel, unsure what she wanted him to do. She didn't say anything, but nodded at him.

He walked over to Zac. "I'm Charlie. Charlie Markowski."

"Zac Keller. Ariel's boss and friend." Zac wanted to hold Nora close and protect her. And as he handed Nora over to Charlie, he felt what amounted to a knife in the heart knowing there was a very real possibility that one day he'd have to do it all over again. He'd have to hand Eli's baby over to Arthur.

And as he stood there, Zac watched as Charlie Markowski fell in love with his daughter.

It was that simple. He'd handed the baby to a boy who, as he held his daughter, turned into a man. The look on Charlie's face said he'd do anything for this baby. And when Charlie glanced up at Ariel, Zac could see that Charlie loved her as well.

Whether it was a love that could overcome all the obstacles they were facing, he wasn't sure. But it was real. And as Charlie walked over to Ariel, and together they gazed at their daughter, that love was a tangible presence in the room.

What if Arthur, who'd spent Eli's pregnancy bouncing back and forth, held his child, fell in love and finally decided he wanted to be a father? What if he convinced Eli to take him back, and to make them a family?

Zac had thought nothing would ever be harder than losing Cessy, but as he looked at the boy, so absolutely in love with a baby he'd spent nine months denying, Zac knew the truth of it. If Arthur came back and took Eli and the baby from him, there wouldn't just be a hole in his heart.

His heart would break.

Zac wasn't sure he'd survive it.

"Ariel, we're going to go and let you and Charlie bond with your baby," Eli said. "You call me if you need anything."

"I will. Thanks, Ms. Cartwright. Eli. Thanks for everything."

"You're welcome, honey." Eli leaned down and kissed Ariel's forehead again.

They all started to walk out of the room but stopped as Ariel called, "Ms. Cartwright. You talked to my parents, right?"

Eli took Zac's hand before she spoke. "I'm sorry, Ariel, but—"

"No, it's okay, Ms. Cartwright. I didn't expect it to make a difference."

"I'll call you tomorrow morning."

"She didn't expect it to make a difference, but she hoped," Tucker said when they'd safely shut the door. "I'd like to kick their asses."

"Got to admit, me, too," Eli said. "But Charlie came. Did you see his face as he looked at Nora? I hope he'll stay involved, even if Ariel and Charlie don't make it as a couple. Babies deserve to know their father."

Zac knew she didn't mean to, but Eli's words hurt. She looked so tired that he didn't have the heart to say anything.

"Eli, are you riding home with me, or…" Tucker paused.

Before Eli could ask to ride with him, Zac said, "I'm going straight into work today, then I'm heading home to sleep, so if you don't mind riding with Tucker?"

"Sure, that's fine." Eli looked confused. "Are you okay?"

"Yeah, I'm fine." But he wasn't. Wasn't at all. The image of Ariel, Charlie and Nora was giving way to one of Eli, Arthur and their baby. Zac tried to shut it out, tried to tell himself he was being foolish, and yet, he couldn't kill his doubts.

"I'll talk to you later," he promised and stalked away.

This was his problem. Not Eli's. His.

And one way or another, he'd fix it.

He just wasn't sure how.

CHAPTER ELEVEN

"The last weeks of a pregnancy are emotional for all moms-to-be, not just teens. There's no way to ignore the fact the baby you carry is a separate and individual person. It moves, it sleeps…it even gets hiccups. The baby is becoming more real by the day, and while that is exciting, you're about to leave behind the life you knew and step into an unknown future."

—*Pregnancy, Childbirth and Parenting for Teens,* by Mary Jeanne Lorei

IT WAS MID-MAY and spring had finally arrived in Western Pennsylvania. After a long winter, it was good to see the sun, to see the landscape green, and it was especially lovely to be able to go out without a coat on every day.

The without-a-coat part was especially

nice for Eli since she hadn't been able to button hers since sometime in April.

Tonight was the last childbirth class.

Somehow that made the fact the baby would arrive in mere weeks seem more real.

Eli said goodbye to their classmates and took a pillow. Zac took the other one and followed her out of the classroom. When they reached the hospital parking lot and got in the car, Zac turned on the radio. They listened to one country song after another on the drive back to Whedon.

The music was loud enough that conversation was all but impossible. And while Eli enjoyed country music, she enjoyed talking to Zac more. The fact that things had been off between them was becoming more and more apparent with each passing day.

They stopped at O'Brien's for their usual after-childbirth class dinner.

"You're very quiet," she said once they'd ordered. Even the thought of eating O'Brien's cheese soup, her current pregnancy craving, couldn't shake her sense of foreboding.

"Just one of those nights." With no subtlety whatsoever, he changed the subject. "How's Ariel?"

"She's doing great. And so's little Nora.

Ariel's eligible to have a tutor until the end of the year. She's planning on attending her graduation ceremony. Every year moves quickly, but this year…?" Her hand rested on her giant stomach. "Maybe it's that I'm pregnant. It just feels surreal that the baby will be here soon. My mom's about ready to burst with excitement."

Her parents had arrived home the week after Ariel delivered, and her mother had tried to make up for lost time and lost shopping by personally buying out every baby store within a twenty-mile radius. "Did I tell you that Mom's already embroidered this gorgeous sampler for the baby's room? She's just waiting to fill in the name."

"That's great," Zac said.

Eli could pinpoint exactly when things had changed. The night Ariel gave birth. What she couldn't pinpoint was what had happened. All she knew was there was a distance between her and Zac.

"Hey, talk to me. Things aren't right, and I don't know why, but… I love you. You made me believe you loved me, too, but lately, I'm not so sure," she tried to explain.

That got his attention. He reached across the table and took her hand. "Eli, you can doubt many things. Frequently lately, I've doubted my own intelligence, but never doubt I love you. I couldn't stop loving you if I tried, and I love the baby. But I—"

"Elinore?" a voice interrupted.

She didn't need to turn to see who was there. To the best of her knowledge, Arthur Stone had never ventured into O'Brien's restaurant. But tonight, he was here.

Of course.

Arthur seemed to have developed a knack for interrupting her life at the most inopportune times.

She tried to think kind thoughts, to feel bad for Arthur and his upset plans, but all she could manage tonight was irritation. She was tired of making excuses for him. Ariel had been right when she said it was just too bad Arthur Stone's life was thrown into chaos with the news of this baby. Eli's had been, too, but she'd managed.

And here he was again, getting between her and Zac.

"Arthur." Her voice sounded colder than she'd meant it to.

He visibly flinched. And Eli couldn't help but notice he looked older. When they'd dated, she'd never really thought of the age difference between them. Now he seemed aged and tired.

She looked at Zac and realized she hadn't given a thought to their age difference in a long time. What had seemed like such a big obstacle didn't matter at all to her now.

"How are you?" Arthur asked.

"I'm fine." When he didn't ask, she added, "So is the baby." Two times Arthur had stood her up for appointments.

"Could we possibly meet sometime next week?" he asked.

"About?" she countered, although she didn't need to. She could almost write Arthur's script. He missed her, and maybe he'd try again to get involved with the baby.

As she stared at him, she knew she didn't want him to try again. She just wanted him gone. She felt guilty, but tried to remind herself what she always told her students: You can't help the way you feel, but you can help the way you act.

"I really need to talk to you. In private." He glanced at Zac, his meaning clear.

She sighed. Arthur's indecisiveness might be driving her crazy, but she saw Zac and knew it was hurting him. She remembered his pain-filled story about Cessy and no longer wondered why he was distant. Of course. He was worried about this…loving the baby and losing it to Arthur. She didn't know how to ease that worry.

She wanted to tell Arthur to get out and leave her and the baby alone. They had Zac. They didn't need Arthur.

But she didn't.

Couldn't.

As much as she'd love to.

"Fine. We can talk. But I'll tell you what I've been telling you all these months. You have two choices. Be a part of the baby's life, or not. There's no longer any choice when it comes to us. Ever."

Arthur didn't respond, but simply said, "I'll call you, then," and left.

Eli loved living in a small town, but at this moment, she'd give anything to be in a big city, where bumping into people just didn't happen like this.

She studied Zac, and knew he was thinking about the baby, about Cessy, about Arthur.

She knew he had to be because she was. "Zac, this is killing you, isn't it?"

"I won't lie. It is. But that night, after I'd told you about Cessy and we made love, I

swore I'd be here for you and the baby. I'm
in this. And I understand that you're connected to Arthur. I don't like it, but I understand it."

"But I'm not. *I'm* not connected to him.
The baby is."

"I know. But Eli, biology might make
someone a father, but never a dad. A dad is
someone who cares. Someone who's going
to be there day in and day out. I don't think
that's ever going to be Arthur."

There was so much pain in Zac's voice,
and it tore at her because she knew she'd put
it there. She'd hurt him. "Zac, I love you."

"And I love you."

"If I could choose, if I had a choice, I'd
pick you to be the baby's father. But I don't
have a choice. I tell the girls all the time, that
life just happens. There are no crib notes to
cheat your way through it. You have to deal
with it as it is. And as it stands, I love you. I
don't love Arthur, but he's the baby's father
and if he wants to be a part of this baby's life,
I'll see to it that he is. Look at what happened
with Charlie and Nora."

Zac visibly flinched as she said the words,
and she felt cruel, but she needed to be clear.
"Once he held his daughter, he fell in love

with her. Maybe that will happen with Arthur. And he should be a part of this baby's life if it does."

She didn't enjoy it, but she knew she'd had to say what she had.

"He's had nothing to do with this baby, but he's the father? What about me? I've been here every step of the way. What am I to this baby? Let's say we get married. And little Junior does something wrong and I want to discipline him. Take away his bike for a week. Will you throw the fact that I'm not his father in my face? Tell me that I don't have the right to discipline him? Will we call Arthur to check that it's okay? I want to be there for all of it. For the big moments, for the small ones. I want to be the baby's dad, but I keep feeling as if you'll never let me."

"Zac, you're not being fair." The waitress came and they both were silent as she placed their orders in front of them.

"Can I get you anything else?" the waitress asked, her chipper voice sounding harsh because she was so obviously happy and they were so obviously unhappy.

"No, thank you," Eli managed to reply. When the waitress left, Eli repeated, "You're not being fair, Zac. If we stay together, certainly, you'd have a say in how the baby was raised, but it won't change the fact that Arthur's involved."

That *if* landed with almost an audible thud. She knew it.

"I know I'm not being fair, damn it. I want to be. I want to be that very cool guy who says, hey, whatever. I'd like to let it all roll off me, and take what I can get. But I'm worth more than just the table scraps in this situation. I want in, Eli. All the way in. No hesitation, no qualifications. I love you and I want to marry you."

Zac didn't give her time to respond, he just continued steamrolling along. "I want us to raise this baby as our own. I want to be the one who takes him out for ice cream to celebrate successes, and the one who sends him to time-out when he makes a mistake. I want to hear about his days at school, I want to worry about him, and I want to blame my grey hair on him. I want to be the one who loves his mother to distraction, and when we kiss, I want him to gag and beg us not to get all mushy in front of him like Tucker does."

"Zac, I want that, too. But no amount of wishing is going to make it so." She looked at him across the table. He was amazing and she'd brought him so much pain. "I think we need a break."

"What? I just told you, I'm in. This situation is no one's fault. It might hurt like hell, but we'll work it all out. I'll be fine."

But he wouldn't. She could see that even if he couldn't. The situation was too reminiscent of his sister's. It was killing him. And she loved him enough to do what he couldn't do. He was right, he was in this. And he'd never walk, no matter how much it tore at him. So, she'd walk for him. She'd walk away from him.

"I don't need a break from us, Eli," he repeated. "I love you."

"You don't understand, I need this," she lied. "The baby's here soon, and it's obvious, I'm not done dealing with Arthur. I know it's hurting you, and to be honest, Zac, I just can't deal with your problems on top of my own."

It was mean, but she also knew if she didn't sound convincing, he'd never let go.

"I need you to give me some space. Let me get my life in order and maybe then…" That was a lie, too. Arthur would always be a part of her life, and she couldn't deal with that fact hurting Zac day after day.

The soup that had sounded so good just a

short while ago was left untouched and forgotten as she stood.

Zac stood as well and his voice was stiff
as he said, "I'll take you home, then."

"It's not far, I'll walk. The baby and I need
the exercise."

She grabbed her purse and coat and started
for the door.

"Eli, please…"

She turned to see the man she loved. "I'm
sorry, Zac. I'm sorry I ever said yes to anything
more than our work sessions. I'm so sorry."

She quickly left the building before she
burst into tears.

She'd hurry home and call Tucker, sure in
the knowledge her friend would comfort her.

A WEEK LATER, ZAC WENT to the front door,
hoping beyond hope it was Eli who was
ringing the doorbell.

He tried to hide his disappointment when
he found Cessy standing on the porch,
glaring at him. "You're a jerk, Zac," she said
by way of salutation as she pushed past him
and entered his apartment.

She stood, ramrod-straight, still glaring at
him.

"You want to sit down?" he offered,

though he wasn't in the mood for listening to his sister's teenage angst.

Truth be told, he wasn't in the mood for much of anything other than being with Eli. He'd picked up the phone and dialed Eli about a hundred times in the last seven days. Every time, he'd hung up before he hit send.

"No, I don't want to come in. I don't want to chat and pretend to be all sympathetic with your plight because I'm not. Not at all."

"Hey, what did I do?"

"Mom was all worried when you didn't come to dinner on Sunday, but I said you were probably too busy with Eli, but you weren't, were you? I stopped at Ariel's and she told me that you broke up with Ms. Cartwright."

"How did Ariel know?"

"Bart heard his mom talking to Ms. Cartwright and got the gist of it. He said something to Ariel."

Zac had forgotten what high school was like. Rumors traveled quicker than the speed of light. "Cessy, I didn't really break up with her, she asked me to back off for a while, and I did."

"Jerk. Idiot. You've always been my hero, but Zac, right now, I'm…" Cessy paused and finally said, "Well, I'm disappointed in you." It was the killer phrase his mother always used to make any of her kids toe the line and do better.

I'm disappointed in you.

The phrase stung.

"She needs you," Cessy said. "That baby needs you."

"The baby has Arthur."

She snorted.

"He wanted another try," Zac stated. "And Eli gave it to him again because he's the baby's biological father."

"Hey, don't play that card with me, Zac. I met the man who biologically fathered me, and I lived with him for six months. I know better that's not what a parent makes. Dad is my father. Not that guy, who by some fluke or broken condom, knocked my mother up. Doesn't matter that this guy's the sperm donor. You can be the baby's father."

"That's not how Eli sees it and that's not how the legal system sees it. Cessy, don't you get it, when we lost you, the whole family had a big gaping hole in it. We missed you. I was your big brother, but I couldn't protect you. The law said that man had a legal right. And it would say the same thing about Arthur."

She shrugged. "So what?"

That wasn't the reaction he expected. "So, I don't think I can go through losing someone I love like that again."

"You've already lost. And the fact that you walked away—" he started to protest, and Cessy quickly amended "—even if she asked you to, means you've really lost. It doesn't matter that Arthur hasn't come to take the baby yet. You're done."

"But—"

"You're so afraid that you're letting the best thing that ever happened to you slip through your fingers." Cessy paused, then quietly, with less heat, said, "You know, all my life, I've looked up to you. I've wanted to be as good and brave a person as my big brother. But now I don't think I want to be. I don't want to be so afraid of losing someone that I wouldn't put up a fight."

"Cessy." She was getting it all wrong. He'd been willing to stay, to fight. He'd gone because Eli asked him. "Cessy," he repeated.

"Cecily, Zac. My big brother, the one I looked up to called me Cessy. You get to call me Cecily."

"Cecily, then. You don't understand."

"Stop. You don't understand, so I'm going to clue you in. Eli didn't ask you to leave because she needed space, she asked you to go because she knew this was hurting you and she loves you enough to want to make that pain stop. But she's as dumb as you are, even if she is a teacher. I'm going to explain this to you slowly, so it has a chance of getting through your extremely thick skull. You. And. Eli. Belong. Together. Everyone knows that, except the two of you. And even if Arthur decides to be a part of this baby's life, you'd still be there, too. You'd be a part of it. Love isn't something that gets smaller if it's divided. That baby will have enough to give some to you and Arthur."

"Cessy—"

"You're being stupid. I know that my leaving was hard on you, that it hurt you, but even if that man had kept me, even if I hadn't come home, I would always have known I was loved. That's a gift. I'd have remembered that. It would have been worth the pain of losing you to have had even one day of your love. How can you not feel that way about Eli and the baby? How can you turn your back on love?"

Zac didn't have an answer.

"These last few days, have you hurt any less?"

He shook his head.

"Well, there you go, Zac." She waved and flounced out.

Zac stood in his foyer mulling over her words.

Was that what he'd done? Had he actually turned his back on love?

CHAPTER TWELVE

"Every student lives for graduation day. A day that marks the transition from childhood to adulthood. Teen mothers marked that transition when they became parents. But that doesn't mean they should stop thinking about graduation and their future. Because, unlike their classmates, their decisions about their future will affect more than themselves, they'll effect their child."

—*Pregnancy, Childbirth and Parenting for Teens,* by Mary Jeanne Lorei

ELI HELD NORA as they sat in the row with the girls from her program. Every time a teen parent graduated, it was a triumph for the girl, for Eli, and it provided a role model for the other students.

Parents and friends filed into the auditorium, and the front dozen or so rows were empty, waiting for the graduates to arrive.

"Your mama's graduating," she whispered in the baby's ear.

Nora didn't pay any attention as she snuggled closer, trying to find a comfortable position against Eli's giant stomach. The baby kicked little Nora.

"Hey, behave," she scolded.

The baby had been much more quiet today than usual, and she found the fact that it had stirred reassuring.

"You don't look very comfortable," came a voice that sent her heartbeat into overdrive. "Maybe I could sit here and help?"

"Zac." She turned and drank in the sight of him. It had been little more than a week. Most days she could believe that they'd figure things out after the baby came and Arthur decided what he was going to do. Somehow, they'd make it work for everyone. But then, the smallest hint of doubt would creep in and she'd worry that she'd lost him. But here he was and for now, that's all that mattered.

"Yeah."

She tried to tell herself that he was here for Ariel because she was part of the CATA

Project. But as he sat in the vacant chair, she didn't believe it. He was here for her.

He didn't have to say a word. The way he reached out and touched her hand, she could tell that he'd needed to connect with her as much as she'd needed to connect with him. She took his hand in hers and held on.

She wasn't sure where her certainty had come from, but she reveled in it.

Zac was back for her.

He held out his free arm and took Nora. Despite the fact she enjoyed holding the baby, there was a sense of relief. Her stomach was so swollen it got in the way of pretty much everything these days. But despite her giant girth and her nagging backache, she felt marvelous. Zac was back.

"Eli, when this is over, could we talk?"

She nodded, not trusting herself to say something without bursting into tears. She'd missed him so much. Had so many things to share. About how the baby was kicking. About how it still seemed to like her right rib, pressing against it all day until by evening it just ached, and she'd sit with a hand on the foot moving it gently away and giving herself some relief.

She wanted to tell him so many things, to share so much of the minutia of her day.

But mainly she wanted to tell Zac that she loved him.

That she wanted to spend the rest of her life loving him.

That no matter what Arthur decided, she was sure Zac would never lose her or the baby. The emotion caught in her throat, preventing anything from coming out.

"Eli, are you okay?" he asked, as he put Nora on his shoulder and gently patted her back.

She nodded again.

"I missed you," he said. "I—"

The music started playing and the senior class began to file into the auditorium from the back. Eli had checked with the principal, and Barry had told her that Ariel would walk down this side of the gym.

She watched as gowned student after gowned student marched by. Soon, Ariel came into view wearing her blue cap and gown, along with her honor society cords.

And suddenly, all that emotion Eli had been trying to rein in, exploded. She could feel the tears streaming down her face, and tried to kneel down and get her purse and the giant stack of tissues she'd packed for just this occasion. The space between the seats didn't leave much room to maneuver herself, but she was managing until she felt a stitch in her back and she let out a sharp gasp.

"Here, let me." Holding Nora in one hand, Zac reached down with his other and retrieved her purse for her.

Eli tried to force herself to breathe normally as she dug for the tissues. In, out. Slow even breaths. It wouldn't do to hyperventilate. This was Ariel's night.

The graduating class had all reached their seats and sat down, then the audience did the same.

"Family and friends, on behalf of myself and the teaching staff, I want to welcome you to this celebration. We are here tonight..." Barry droned.

Eli had sat through years and years of graduations. She'd always felt a bit misty as she watched girls from her program graduate. But Ariel's graduation was special.

She reached over and touched Nora's peach-fuzzy hair, but stopped short because her back twinged again.

"Eli, are you sure you're all right?"

"I did something to my back. Probably just the stress of carrying all this extra weight."

He didn't look convinced.

"I'm fine, Zac. Really, I'm fine."

He gently held her hand as the baby slept and the various speakers came and went. Then one by one the graduates walked across the stage, received their diplomas, shook hands with Barry, then moved their tassels from the right side to the left.

"Laurel Lee."

"C. J. Manto."

"Charlie Markowski." Nora's father walked across the stage. He'd been true to his word in the hospital, helping with the baby and helping financially. Ariel had confessed they were dating again, though she'd qualified that most of their dates involved things for the baby. A trip to the zoo, a walk in the evening.

"Ariel Mayor." Ariel made her way across the stage, and like everyone before her, took her diploma and shook the principal's hand, then walked across the stage, turned to face the audience and moved her tassel from one side to the other.

Eli clapped until her hands hurt, but she didn't care. Ariel was her only graduating student this year, which just added to the specialness of the evening.

When the final diploma had been handed out and the ceremony ended, Ariel came to find them. "Thanks for being here, Ms. Cartwright and Mr. Keller. I saw Aunt Deirdre and I need to go find her, but I wanted to say thank you to you both."

Eli didn't ask about Ariel's parents, and neither did Zac. At least her aunt had made it.

"Congratulations, Ariel. We're both so proud of you."

"I brought something with me." Zac shifted Nora and took an envelope out of his pocket. "Keller's Market is proud to give you our first CATA scholarship to the college of your choice. If you pick one in town or nearby, you'll have a job with us throughout. If you choose a college farther afield, I have connections. I'll help you find another job with someone who will work with you."

Ariel opened the envelope and read the note then started to cry. "Mr. Keller, you don't know how much this means to me. To us. I—" She gave up trying to talk and hugged him, sandwiching Nora between them.

"Here, let me rescue the baby." Charlie took the baby from Zac and rather than ending her hug, it allowed Ariel to hold on longer.

When she finally broke free, she turned to Eli and hugged her as well. "Ms. Cartwright, I know that teachers are paid to be here and that it's not an easy job even if you stick to the job description and present lessons and grade papers. But you, you go even further. You cared about me. When I walked across that stage and took my diploma from Principal Werner's hands, it was because of you."

Eli felt the tears welling up in her eyes again and started digging through her purse for tissues. "Ariel, I just—"

"No. Don't. You're going to try and tell me it was nothing, that it was your job. But Ms. Cartwright, it was everything to me. And I know that I was more than a job to you. That all the girls in the program are more than a job. And I got accepted to Mercyhurst. They have a great education program. For a long time I didn't know what I wanted to do when I grew up. Having Nora forced me to grow up faster than most kids, and having you as a teacher made me know what I want to do. I'm going to be a teacher. Someday, I want to impact someone else's life the way you've impacted mine. You are what every teacher should be, Ms. Cartwright. Thank you."

Eli tried to say something, tried to make

words form, but all she could do was moan as another spasm hit her back.

"Ms. Cartwright?" Ariel asked at the same time that Zac said, "Eli?" There was concern in both their voices.

"I think that maybe the back pain I've been having all day is more than a pulled muscle."

"Back labor. I remember you taught us about that," Ariel said. "I didn't have it."

"But I think I am. And I really think I need to go to the hospital. I'm sorry to cancel our dinner, Ariel."

"Come on, Ms. Cartwright, this is so much more important."

The pain subsided, and Eli gently touched Ariel's cheek with her finger. "Ariel, you are important to me, and we're going to take a rain check, okay? This day deserves to be celebrated."

"Yes, it does," Zac agreed.

"I'll be taking Ariel and her aunt out now, Ms. Cartwright," Charlie said, "and you guys can take her sometime after your baby's here, okay?" Still holding Nora, Charlie wrapped his free arm around Ariel.

"Thanks, Charlie." Looking at the three of them, Eli recognized a family in the making and though she knew odds were stacked against them, she hoped that Ariel and Charlie would make it.

"Come on Eli, let's go." Zac took her arm as if she couldn't manage by herself. She was about to tell him that she could, when another pain hit and she gratefully leaned on him.

"Hey, Mr. Keller, will you call me?" Ariel called.

"Sure." He dropped his voice and said, "Let's get you out of here before you have your baby on the floor."

"It would be a graduation first," Eli joked, smiling through the pain.

ZAC WASN'T SOME BIG-GAME hunter, and he'd never thought it overly prudent to bungee-jump or sky-dive, but still he thought that when it came to bravery he had an ample amount. Instead, as he raced through the bustling downtown traffic to the hospital, he felt panic.

"Zac, how much longer?"

Eli had asked him that question countless times between Whedon and Erie. Finally, he was able to say, "Only a couple more minutes. I can see the hospital."

"Good. The E.R. entrance is in the back." Her voice was breathy.

"You okay?" He'd lost precious time because he'd been stupid enough to let Eli push him away. He should never have listened to her, or left. He should have stuck to her regardless.

"I'm fine," she managed to say.

Thankfully there were valets in the parking lot. Zac tossed them his keys, and took the slip, before helping Eli inside.

A nurse settled her into a wheelchair so she could escort them to the obstetrics floor.

"Well, Zac, thanks for everything."

Zac realized he'd never told her what he'd planned on telling her.

"Eli, I'd like to come…if you want me. I want to be here for you. I came tonight to talk, but I don't think right now is the best time. But please, let me stay. We'll talk later."

He was afraid she'd say no, but he could see the relief on her face. "Thank you."

While the nurses prepped Eli, he called her parents.

"We're on our way in," her mother told him. "It would be nice if you'd at least stay with her until we get there."

There was a coldness in her mother's voice that had never been there before.

"I'm not going anywhere, Mrs. Cartwright. I planned on telling Eli after the graduation, but other things took precedence."

Just like that, her mother warmed. "I knew you'd work it out. I tried to understand why she did it, but still, I felt she'd been hasty and told her so."

"Maybe, but it was even worse that I listened and went anyway. I worked out a lot of things last week, ma'am."

"Things you probably should tell Eli before me." Eli's mother laughed. "We'll be there soon. I'm glad you'll be staying, Zac."

He'd be staying for a lot longer than the delivery if he had his way. He was just about bursting with the need to tell Eli his feelings, but he knew right now she had other things to concentrate on. "I'll look after her, Mrs. Cartwright."

"Let me be the first to welcome you to the family, Zac. I knew you'd be a part of it when I saw the way you looked at my daughter that first time I met you, right after she told us about the baby. That look…that's why I wasn't sure if the baby's was yours or Arthur's. You mean a lot to Eli, and I'm sure you'll mean a lot to this baby, too."

Eli's mother's words meant so much. "Thanks, Mrs. Cartwright. I—"

The nurse interrupted. "Mr. Keller, Eli's asking for you now."

"Mrs. Cartwright, I have to go." He snapped his phone shut and hurried into the room. "I texted Tucker, and I called your mom."

"Great. She's so—"

Another pain hit and began a cycle of contractions and breathing, brief rests, then back at it again. He fed Eli an occasional ice chip, helped her concentrate on breathing, but basically felt useless. He hated to see her in pain.

The nurse told him that back labors tended to be more intense, and helped them position Eli more comfortably. But more comfortably wasn't nearly comfortable enough in Zac's opinion. When they offered her pain meds, Eli insisted that she didn't want to miss a moment.

Eventually, her doctor came in and after checking Eli assured them it was time.

Zac very thankfully remained by Eli's head, and well out of the viewing range as he continued to play cheerleader. "Breathe, Eli… Huff. Huff. Huff."

"I can see the baby's head. This one's got a full head of hair, Mom," the doctor said. "Don't push, Eli. Let me just ease the baby's shoulders through. Breathe. Breathe."

Zac breathed along with her, huffing in hopes of controlling the urge to push.

"There, you're good," Dr. Benton said. "Push the next time you have the urge."

There was no waiting. Eli pushed and cried out as she flopped back on the pillow.

A minute later, the doctor cried, "It's a boy!" And as if on cue, the baby wailed. The doctor held the baby aloft and placed him on Eli's chest. "Would you like to cut the umbilical cord, Dad?"

Zac didn't know how to respond, so he looked at Eli. "Zac? Only if you want."

"I want."

He followed the doctor's instructions, made the cut and realized that this baby, who'd been a part of Eli for nine long months was now a separate person in his own right. This tiny little boy would learn to walk and talk. He'd go to school. Maybe play sports. He'd learn to drive.

And Zac wanted to be there for every new skill, every milestone.

He wanted to tell Eli and her son all of that

and more, but there were just too many words, too many emotions, so he simply settled for, "I love you. I love you both."

"We love you, Zac. I know there's still things to say and there's Arthur—"

"You should probably call him," he suggested, more because he needed her to see he was going to be able to handle Arthur.

"Sir, maybe you'd be more comfortable waiting outside for a minute while we freshen up Eli and the baby?" the nurse asked.

"I could call if you want," he offered. He'd accepted that he was going to have to deal with Arthur for the rest of his life, since he intended it to be that way with Eli. He might as well get started with doing it the right away.

"Really?" Eli studied him, then nodded. "His number's in my cell, which is in my purse."

"You do ask a lot from a man, Eli," he teased. "I mean, going in your purse is the job for only a very brave man."

She smiled. "I really do love you, Zac Keller."

ELI HAD NEVER BEEN so tired in her life, and conversely, she'd never felt more alive. Her parents had come and seen the baby. It was all her father could do to pull her mom back out the door, and the only way he managed that was with Eli's assurance she'd need her mother's help when she went home the following day.

Zac had sat on the couch in the birthing room and had dozed off within minutes of her parents leaving. That left Eli plenty of time to watch him sleep. They still hadn't talked about what his being here meant, but she hoped that he was back to stay because he'd come to terms with the situation.

There was a knock at the door, which startled Zac awake. The baby stirred as well. "Shh," she whispered, then called softly, "Come in."

Arthur stuck his head into the room and for a moment, she thought he was going to bolt.

Instead, he stepped all the way in. "He called me." He nodded toward Zac. "I thought I should come."

Eli studied the man she'd once thought she'd loved and realized he'd never shared himself with her the way Zac had.

Zac had told her about the day they'd taken Cessy away. He'd given her son his piggy bank, which represented so much more that a place to save money—it had been a place Zac had saved his dreams. She wanted nothing more than to tell Zac everything she was feeling, but first there was Arthur.

He stood at the very end of her bed, looking at the baby.

"Arthur, would you like to see my son?" she asked. She untucked the blanket and moved the baby so he was facing the ceiling rather than turned toward her.

She saw Zac get up off the couch. "I should go."

"No, please. I need you." She wasn't trying to be cruel. She needed him here. She needed him to hear.

She could see from his expression that he thought staying would be awkward, but she'd said she needed him and so he stayed. "Okay."

Eli had known that Zac loved her, but how had she not known the second she had met him that she loved him?

Arthur eyed Zac, then addressed Eli, and finally the baby. "I thought about buying him something. It seemed that a father should bring a son a gift."

She could see Zac wince, but because he

was behind Arthur, her ex didn't notice, and even if he had, she doubted he'd have cared. "But then it occurred to me that I don't feel like his father. I thought maybe when I got here and saw him that there would be some magic link. But there's not. I don't feel anything for him. You were right when you called him your son. He's yours Eli. I wish I was a better man, one who could stand by you and at least pretend this was what I wanted, but I can't. I don't want to be anyone's father."

He reached into his suit jacket's inner pocket. "Here are the papers. They're signed. And there's my lawyer's number along with some basics on the trust I'm setting up for him. You're supposed to call my lawyer with his name when you know it."

"I already know it. I'm naming him after my father and his father." She looked pointedly at Zac. "Jonathan Zachary Cartwright."

She saw the words impact on Zac. She remembered what Cessy had said at dinner… that she could talk to Zac without words. And right now, she didn't need words to know he was touched, and that he had taken to Johnny as his son long before she gave him his name.

Zac loved them both.

He'd come today even though he knew that Arthur might decide to stay. He'd come because he cared about them more than he worried about his own pain.

"Jonathan Zachary Cartwright Keller," Zac corrected. "That is if you both will have me."

It was a proposal. And maybe in any other circumstances, proposing while someone's ex was standing there would have been bad form, but given everything they'd been through, it was fine.

She nodded.

Arthur looked at the three of them. "Good luck, Eli. I wish you all the best."

He kissed her lightly on the cheek, then turned to Zac. "You'll take care of them?"

"They're my family," Zac said simply, moving to Eli's side. "I figured it out. We match."

Arthur seemed confused, but Eli got it. She understood. "We match perfectly," she assured him.

"I'll let the three of you bond then, as all the books mention."

Eli looked surprised.

"Elinore, I'm an academic, I read up on the process. And I get it now."

"Get what, Arthur?" she asked.

He stood still, studying the three of them. "Get why I never felt a connection to this child…because I was never really his father."

Arthur turned and when he opened the door, Zac called, "Arthur, if you want to know how he is, if you want to check…"

Arthur glanced over his shoulder and shook his head. "I won't, but thanks. Just take care of them."

He left, and Eli focused on the man she loved.

Zac had one hand on her, one on Johnny. "You do realize that when I said his name would be Jonathan Zachary Cartwright Keller, I was asking you to marry me?"

"Elinore Cartwright-Keller. It has a nice ring." She picked up the baby and held him out to Zac. "Johnny, meet your father. Zac, your son."

Zac took the baby in his arms. Johnny was a bit red-looking, but Zac had only ever seen one thing more beautiful. He looked at Eli— so beautiful.

"Eli, remember at Christmas when you gave me that painting and I said it was the best gift I'd ever received?"

How could she forget. "Yes."

"I lied." His voice was husky with emotion. "You are. Johnny is."

"That's two things," she joked.

"No, it's not," Zac argued. "You and Johnny are one—a family. My family. Our family. We all match."

EPILOGUE

"Delivering your baby might seem as if it should be the end of the book, but there are still more chapters left. Because carrying and having a baby is the easy part. Raising that child, creating your own family…those are lessons you never stop learning."

—*Pregnancy, Childbirth and Parenting for Teens,* by Mary Jeanne Lorei

ARIEL JIGGLED NORA on her knee and saw that Mrs. Cartwright, Eli's mom, was doing the same thing with Johnny. Both babies had reached a crawling-all-over age that made them less than happy about sitting through a marriage ceremony.

But Ariel had seen Mrs. Cartwright dab at her eyes, just as she'd dabbed at her own as Eli and Zac said their vows in front of a church filled with friends and family. Even

Tucker, who was wearing a dress and standing next to Eli as her maid of honor, was misty-eyed.

"And I promise to stand by you through it all. You and Johnny are my world, my heart, my life," Zac vowed.

Cecily and Mrs. Keller burst into noisy tears, the rest of the Keller family looked on the verge of crying as well.

"I, Elinore, take you, Zachary, for better and worse. You came to me at one of the most confusing times in my life, and you gave me the strength to find a new path. Once I found it, it made sense that you were there, walking alongside of me. Wherever we go, I know I'll be just fine as long as you're there. I'm a teacher, but it took me until recently to figure out that life just happens… I didn't plan any of this, but I'm so lucky to have found it. To have found you. I love you, Zac…."

Charlie took Ariel's hand and squeezed it.

He'd asked her to marry him, but Ariel had said no. For now, it was enough that he was in her life, that he wanted to be a father to Nora. They were both still young. Maybe someday, when they were older, when they were sure they were marrying for the right reasons, but she wouldn't marry because it seemed convenient. And not just for Nora's sake. She wanted a family who matched. So, maybe someday…

For now though, Ariel would revel in Zac and Eli's wedding and enjoy the day. Tomorrow she had to go back to juggling her daughter, her college classes and work.

But it was worth it because Ariel had direction.

In a few years she was going to be a teacher like Elinore Cartwright-Keller and be a positive influence in her students' lives like Eli had with her kids.

That thought, that goal, was enough to get Ariel through the hardest moments. She was going to take it one day at a time because like Ms. Cartwright had said, life just happens. There were no crib notes for it.

* * * * *

*Celebrate 60 years of pure reading
pleasure with Harlequin®!
Just in time for the holidays,
Silhouette Special Edition®
is proud to present*
New York Times *bestselling author
Kathleen Eagle's*
ONE COWBOY, ONE CHRISTMAS

Rodeo rider Zach Beaudry was a
travelin' man—until he broke down in
middle-of-nowhere South Dakota during a deep freeze. That's when an angel
came to his rescue….

"Don't die on me. Come on, Zel. You know how much I love you, girl. You're all I've got. Don't do this to me here. Not *now*."

But Zelda had quit on him, and Zach Beaudry had no one to blame but himself. He'd taken his sweet time hitting the road, and then miscalculated a shortcut. For all he knew he was a hundred miles from gas. But even if they were sitting next to a pump, the ten dollars he had in his pocket wouldn't get him out of South Dakota, which was not where he wanted to be right now. Not even his beloved pickup truck, Zelda, could get him much of anywhere on fumes. He was sitting out in the cold in the middle of nowhere. And getting colder.

He shifted the pickup into Neutral and pulled hard on the steering wheel, using the downhill slope to get her off the blacktop and into the roadside grass, where she shuddered to a standstill. He stroked the padded dash. "You'll be safe here."

But Zach would not. It was getting dark, and it was already too damn cold for his cowboy ass. Zach's battered body was a barometer, and he was feeling South Dakota, big time. He'd have given his right arm to be climbing into a hotel hot tub instead of a brutal blast of north wind. The right was his free arm anyway. Damn thing had lost altitude, touched some part of the bull and caused him a scoreless ride last time out.

It wasn't scoring him a ride this night, either. A carload of teenagers whizzed by, topping off the insult by laying on the horn as they passed him. It was at least twenty minutes before another vehicle came along. He stepped out and waved both arms this time, damn near getting himself killed. Whatever happened to *do unto others?* In places like this, decent people didn't leave each other stranded in the cold.

His face was feeling stiff, and he figured he'd better start walking before his toes went numb. He struck out for a distant yard light, the only sign of human habitation in sight. He couldn't tell how distant, but he knew he'd be hurting by the time he got there, and he was counting on some kindly old man to be answering the door. No shame among the lame.

It wasn't like Zach was fresh off the operating table—it had been a few months since his last round of repairs—but he hadn't given himself enough time. He'd lopped a couple of weeks off the near end of the doc's estimated recovery time, rigged up a brace, done some heavy-duty taping and climbed onto another bull. Hung in there for five seconds—four seconds past feeling the pop in his hip and three seconds short of the buzzer.

He could still feel the pain shooting down his leg with every step. Only this time he had to pick the damn thing up, swing it forward and drop it down again on his own.

Pride be damned, he just hoped *somebody* would be answering the door at the end of the road. The light in the front window was a good sign.

The four steps to the covered porch might as well have been four hundred, and he was looking to climb them with a lead weight chained to his left leg. His eyes were just as screwed up as his hip. Big black spots danced around with tiny red flashers, and he couldn't tell what was real and what wasn't. He stumbled over some shrubbery, steadied himself on the porch railing and peered between vertical slats.

There in the front window stood a spruce tree with a silver star affixed to the top. Zach was pretty sure the red sparks were all in his head, but the white lights twinkling by the hundreds throughout the huge tree, those were real. He wasn't too sure about the woman hanging the shiny balls. Most of her hair was caught up on her head and fastened in a curly clump, but the light captured by the escaped bits crowned her with a golden halo. Her face was a soft shadow, her body a willowy silhouette beneath a long white gown. If this was where the mind ran off to when cold started shutting down the rest of the body, then Zach's final worldly thought was, *This ain't such a bad way to go*.

If she would just turn to the window, he could die looking into the eyes of a Christmas angel.

* * * * *

*Could this woman from Zach's past get
the lonesome cowboy to come in
from the cold…for good?*

Look for
ONE COWBOY, ONE CHRISTMAS
by Kathleen Eagle
Available December 2009 from
Silhouette Special Edition®

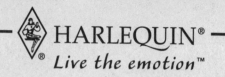

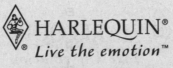

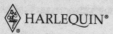

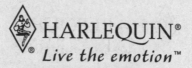

HARLEQUIN®
INTRIGUE®

BREATHTAKING ROMANTIC SUSPENSE

Shared dangers and passions lead to electrifying
romance and heart-stopping suspense!

Every month, you'll meet six new heroes
who are guaranteed to make your spine tingle
and your pulse pound. With them you'll enter
into the exciting world of Harlequin Intrigue—
where your life is on the line
and so is your heart!

THAT'S INTRIGUE—
ROMANTIC SUSPENSE
AT ITS BEST!

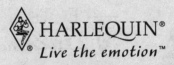

HARLEQUIN®
Live the emotion™

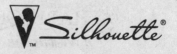

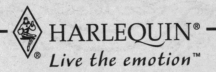

Harlequin® Historical
Historical Romantic Adventure!

*Imagine a time of chivalrous
knights and unconventional ladies,
roguish rakes and impetuous
heiresses, rugged cowboys
and spirited frontierswomen—
these rich and vivid tales will
capture your imagination!*

*Harlequin Historical . . .
they're too good to miss!*

HHDIR06